The Quiet Rebel

By the same author

Scandal's Daughter
Reasons of the Heart

The Quiet Rebel

JOANNA ERLE

ROBERT HALE · LONDON

© Joanna Erle 2003
First published in Great Britain 2003

ISBN 0 7090 7496 4

Robert Hale Limited
Clerkenwell House
Clerkenwell Green
London EC1R 0HT

The right of Joanna Erle to be identified as
author of this work has been asserted by her
in accordance with the Copyright, Designs and
Patents Act 1988.

2 4 6 8 10 9 7 5 3 1

Typeset in 11/14½ Souvenir by
Derek Doyle & Associates, Liverpool.
Printed in Great Britain by
St Edmundsbury Press, Bury St Edmunds, Suffolk.
Bound by Woolnough Bookbinding Limited.

For Bruce

Author's Note

There is no village of Elswick lying between Pagham and Selsey, but the Elswick I have created is representative of many small coastal villages in Sussex and Kent at the time of the Coastal Blockade when the government was determined to put down smuggling on which many villages between Chichester and Deal depended for survival.

J. E.

'We are told to forgive our enemies;
we are not told to forgive our friends.'

Bacon

Prologue

1807

The boy watched the sloop tack the last of the distance towards Elswick's small harbour, his gaze fixed on the tall, fair-headed helmsman. As the *Euniki* glided through the harbour entrance, the young man glanced up, his vividly blue gaze meeting the dark intensity of the child's. A moment later he raised his hand in greeting.

His wonder and pleasure in that acknowledgement robbed Nick of his chance to respond. The *Euniki* had gone by and was turning in to her usual berth, her sails rattling to their resting places to be neatly furled back by the crew. He raced back along the jetty to wait by the iron ladder on the harbour wall while the sloop was made fast and the fair-haired man gave a few last directions to the others before climbing the ladder.

From gazing down, Nick now gazed up sharply, dwarfed by the man's size.

'Master Nicholas Mariott, isn't it?' he was asked, in a voice lightly touched by a Sussex burr.

Nick nodded. Added shyly, 'My friends call me Nick.'

The young man's smile broadened. 'Oh. Am I a friend?'

Dare he claim so much? Nick drew breath; offered, 'If you please, sir.'

'Don't *sir* me, lad. I'm plain Joshua Ryland and *my* friends call me Josh. So Nick and Josh it is.' He held out a hand.

Putting a very much smaller one into it, Nick was speechless, though his mind was exulting, *Nick and Josh!* Joshua Ryland, 22 years old, owner of the *Euniki*, notable seaman, notable smuggler, was his *friend. . . .*

Looking at the boy's rapt expression, Josh's own expression sobered, sensing that, without intention, he had taken on a responsibility. He said, 'Well, Nick, if you've nothing better to do, you could walk me to the door of the Sussex Oak. I've some business to discuss with Ben Saulter.'

No consideration of time or commitment could have prevented Nick falling in beside his new-found friend. What they talked of on their way to the inn, Nick was never to remember, but when, at the open door of the inn they parted, he carried away Josh Ryland's parting words like a trophy, 'Goodbye, friend Nick, until next time we meet.'

From there, Nick raced back to the harbour. All but a small part of the *Euniki*'s catch would probably have been unloaded at Chichester or elsewhere; by the time he reached the jetty he expected the landsmen would be scrubbing out her empty hold. He would watch that with all the interest of an exacting owner.

Ben Saulter, landlord of the Sussex Oak, turned from laying another log on the driftwood fire and smiled as Josh ducked his head under the lintel.

'Good catch, Josh?'

'Can't complain.'

'Was that the Mariott boy with you?'

'Yes. Just now in want of a friend, it seems, for all that he'll own most of Elswick and a good deal else one day.'

'Doesn't surprise me. Shouldn't think that father of his has

12

much time for a nine year old. Bullies him, I've heard. His mother's death last year must have come hard to the lad.' He dusted his hands on his breeches. 'Now, what are you drinking?'

CHAPTER ONE

1826

'What we anticipate seldom occurs;
what we least expect generally happens.'
Benjamin Disraeli.

'God-dammit, Josh, will you *listen*! They could hang you! Even if only as a deterrent to others. You wouldn't be the first free-trader to go that way.'

Strung between exasperation and despairing affection, Nick glared at the man sitting on the other side of the inn table. Neither persuasion nor argument was making any headway against the good-humoured obstinacy of the man who for close on twenty years had been his friend, and at need, surrogate father and older brother. Time had taken nothing from his splendid physique; had only faintly hazed the brightness of his thick, waving hair.

'First, as I've already said, they have to catch me.' Josh let the ever-ready smile broaden on his face, crinkling the laughter lines around his blue eyes. He shook his head at Nick. 'Don't fret so, lad.'

At ten in the morning they were the only occupants of the Sussex Oak's taproom. The smell of damp wood and lye-soap rose strongly from the recently scrubbed tables mingling with the pleasanter scent of burning wood given off by the fire that sent a warm glimmer through the wide, low-ceilinged room. For all that it was August, the morning glimpsed through the latticed window and the open door showed coldly grey.

'It's no joke, Josh,' Nick snapped back. 'The government's set on putting down smuggling and using the navy to do it. There will be twenty men or more here in Elswick to watch every move anyone makes. Men trained to the sea, trained to fight. Government and navy have to win in the end.'

The blue gaze lost its smile. 'What hasn't been said is what those who work with me will do for a living if I stop. Can you employ them all, keep their families fed, hosed and shod? Those who've lived comfortably aren't going to take easily to starving on tuppence ha'penny a day charity money. And that's the up and the down of it, Nick Mariott.'

'What will any of it matter if you turn Elswick into a battle-ground? You could end with blood on your hands, Josh Ryland.'

'Oughtn't you have said *innocent* blood?' For the first time anger speared through Josh's easy good-temper.

'So it well may be!' Nick's patience was slipping too, and he ventured on to dangerous ground. 'What about your boys? Andy's fifteen. Growing up. You've kept him away from smuggling so far, but for how much longer?'

'Leave my sons to me. They're no concern of yours.' There was an ominous growl in the warning.

His family. . . . Josh's Achilles' heel, as Nick well knew. The silence that followed lay heavily on them before Josh spoke again the warning note still in his voice. 'Through the years, you and me, we've never had cause to quarrel. And there was a time when you saw things different.'

'A time when I wanted to be one of you? I was a boy – a child – with less sense than I might have had.'

Josh swept that aside. 'Maybe so. But what I do I was born to. There's no man among those who sail with me held against his will, bound by threats of fearful punishment as some in the trade

15

are. But I'll stop when *I* choose, Nick. Which isn't now when the market's hungrier than ever.' With a hint of malice, he added, 'If I *did* stop, it wouldn't be long before you lost half your rents. You thought of that?'

'Yes. And beyond. But have *you* thought you could be betrayed by someone wanting to save their own skin?'

'Chance it might happen. Chance I could drown at sea any day. But enough's been said. What it comes down to is that you're letting a naval shore-party on to your land and I'm not giving up smuggling to make things easy for you.'

Nick's patience broke. 'Damn you, Josh – you're a fool! What I'd like at this moment is to up-end what's left in this pot over your stubborn head!'

'You'd be sorry.' Suddenly there was a distance between them that had never been there before. Then, with black and flagrant intent, Josh added, 'Great man though you be these days.'

Cold, savage rage blasted through Nick. In a voice that cut like a whip, he said, 'Never before have I thought of you as less than my equal, Joshua Ryland. More often than not, I have believed you the better man. I see now I was wrong on both counts.'

The pause was no longer than between the flash from a gun and the bullet striking home before Josh loomed to his feet, as lean, lithe and powerful as twenty years ago. Now a threat made visible, he laid his hands palm-down on the table as though to keep them from use. 'Damn you to hell! You've made clear where you stand and I've done the same.' His slight accent thickened to parody. 'What comes of that we'll need have to abide. Won't we, *Mister* Mariott?' Turning about, he strode out of the inn.

Nick gazed blindly after him. The gibe *Great man though you be*. . . . had been unjustifiable. Unforgivable. He had thought their friendship indestructible. His mistake. What, after all, did Josh owe him?

He thought bitterly of the likely effect on Elswick of Josh's determination to carry on smuggling. It seemed that he was now fated to stand by and watch calamity come down on the village like one of the seven plagues of Egypt. A plague from which Elswick would emerge, after suffering who-knew-what individual tragedies, as just another poverty-stricken Sussex village with half its people barely scratching a living and the other half sunk in despairing beggary.

Walking back to Danesfield, his thoughts remained bleak. James, the footman, opening the door, took a surprised second look at his master's face. Young Mr Mariott, unlike his father, Jack Mariott, was known as an easy-going man, but that was not his look at the moment.

Hardly aware of the man's presence, Nick walked through the hall into his bookroom. Closing the door, he crossed immediately to a side table and poured himself a brandy, an unusual recourse at this morning hour. He tossed it down as little aware of doing so as he had been aware of his footman.

How long he sat behind his desk before he became conscious of a light tapping on the door of the room he did not know. Reluctantly, he called, 'Come.'

The mixture of emotions on his young godson's face as he came in pushed him into making an effort to give the boy his attention. 'Well, Henry,' he said, 'what now?'

'Er . . . good morning Uncle Nick. I came over to. . . . Well, the thing is, I thought you might. . . .' Henry came to a halt a yard or two from the writing-table, straightened his shoulders and brought out in a rush, 'I've brought you a – a kind of present. James is holding it in the hall.'

'Because it's so large? So heavy?'

'Oh, no. It's about the usual size. Well, I think it is.' He traced one of the arabesques in the Aubusson carpet with a booted foot and looked hopefully at Nick.

'You relieve my mind. But what have I done to merit even a *kind* of present outside Christmas and my birthday?'

'Well, I thought *you* might like to have it. It's just that. . . .' He stuck on that.

17

'You want to be rid of it?'

'No, I don't!' His tone rose indignantly. 'It's Aunt Amelia who does. She made Uncle Matthew tell Kibble to get rid of him because he kept her awake all night. I didn't hear him!'

'Ah. . . . Now we're a little closer to the mystery. The object is alive and of the male gender, normal size you think, and not too big for James to hold. Suppose you tell me now the exact nature of this gift that disturbs your aunt's nights. I take it you think it – he? – won't disturb mine?'

Henry looked anxious. 'Not if you keep him in the house. He's a dog.'

'Now I begin to understand. What breed? That is if he *has* any breeding.'

Henry advanced an eager step or two. 'Oh, yes, he has. He's quite splendid, truly he is. He's a Dalmatian. A *smiling* Dalmatian. They don't all smile you know. I had him from Sir Roland Anstey's groom, Bratby. He breeds them. But this one was left over from a litter because someone trod on his tail and it mended with a kink. Only a *small* kink, but I got him cheaply because of it. I call him Dotty because he's dotted.'

Nick found a smile for the boy. 'Very original,' he said. 'And is he dotty in the doited sense?'

'Well, a bit. He's only seven months. If he'd had time to grow into sense he wouldn't have made a racket. But Aunt Amelia made me shut him in the stables and he howled because he'd got used to sleeping in my room and probably felt lonely.'

'Sleeping on your bed, was he?'

'Well, yes. But I'd only had him a week and I didn't know he'd been out in the rain that last time and that his paws were muddy. It isn't fair! But I thought if *you* had him, I could come and see him and take him out for you. Bratby said he'd make a prime carriage-dog when he's full grown and even a useful gun dog if he proves to have a nose.'

'Yes. I can see that to have a smiling Dalmatian – even one with a kink in his tail – running between the rear wheels of my carriage

18

would add a degree of consequence to my style. One must hope it would not put our neighbours too completely in the shade.'

'Well, it would, wouldn't it?' Henry agreed innocently. 'I mean, Mrs Timson's new carriage would be nothing to it!'

Nick's lips twitched. 'I think it's time I saw this ornamental animal, don't you?'

Henry sped out of the room and returned even more quickly towed by a large and very handsome Dalmatian who smirked ingratiatingly at Nick, revealing a splendid set of teeth. Not waiting for an introduction, still towing Henry with him, the dog rounded the desk to make his own impetuous advances. Enduring the assault for a moment or two, Nick then commanded the animal to sit and Dotty, recognizing authority, obliged.

Henry beamed. 'You see! He *is* learning. I've been training him.'

'Yes,' Nick agreed, suspecting Bratby might have had more than a little to do with it. Even more mendaciously, he went on, 'Not to confuse him I suggest he remains yours and lives with me as a kind of permanent house-guest. And since I am to have the – er – pleasure of his company it seems to me only fair that I should pay half his purchase price.'

This was beyond any expectations Henry had entertained and he said doubtfully, 'Do you think so? I was going to give him to you.'

'A kind thought, Henry, but I think my suggestion fairer all round. So how much did you pay for him?'

'Five guineas.'

Even with a damaged tail, Bratby could have asked anyone for a great deal more than that: the dog was a splendid specimen. Well done, Bratby, Nick thought; he would see that the man did not lose by it.

Accepting the coins Nick held out to him, Henry handed over the leash he held and sternly bade Dotty be good. Dotty looked at him and smiled enigmatically. Dredging his mind for something to offer in return, Henry recalled a small item of news.

'There's a cousin of Uncle Matthew's coming to stay with us soon,' he said. 'Well, I 'spose she's my cousin, too. Her name's Elise Hilliard. Aunt Amelia isn't best pleased. She said something about her being ruined and if she needed somewhere to hide herself why did it have to be here. She said, too, how very bad the scandal must be that even if she *does* have a fortune she hadn't caught herself a husband.' He looked at Nick with puzzled enquiry. 'How can a lady be ruined if she has a fortune? Because that means she *does* have some money, doesn't it?'

Nick regarded him thoughtfully for a moment then said without inflection, 'There are other ways to be ruined. It can mean to lose one's good name. Like being caught cheating at cards and no one wanting to know you afterwards.'

'Do you think that's what Miss Hilliard did?'

'It's possible, but unlikely, I think. But a gentleman should not discuss a lady's reputation. I suspect you were not supposed to hear what your aunt said, so take care not to repeat it to anyone else.'

'No, I won't. But if a lady doesn't cheat at cards, what else could she cheat at?'

Nick paused for thought before saying, 'That's a wide open question, Henry. But as I said, gentlemen don't discuss a lady's reputation, so we won't go into it any further just now. Now run along. I'll keep Dotty with me so that he can begin to accustom himself to his change of abode. Come tomorrow and see how he's doing. After that you may take him out whenever you're free of your lessons with the Reverend Staunton. They begin again on Thursday, don't they?'

His attention diverted, Henry nodded. 'And thanks, Uncle Nick. You're a trump.' His tone was fervently grateful but he added anxiously, 'You will keep him in the house, won't you?'

'For my sins, I will.'

Dotty rose to his feet as Henry headed for the door and lunged the length of his lead. He uttered one sharp, protesting bark as the door closed on the boy and then turned an intelligent and enquiring eye on Nick.

'For better or worse, you live here now,' Nick told him severely 'but you will not be sleeping on my bed. What is more, a change of name will be made as soon as the time is ripe.'

Dotty might almost have understood. He did more than smile – he grinned.

Nick found himself nodding at the animal. 'Don't over-reach yourself, my friend. Though I suspect you are exactly what young Henry needs and Bratby deserves your full value for recognizing it.'

Not for the first time, he reflected how much he would like to wring Amelia Woodstow's rigid neck. Her narrow, bloodless nature made it more than unfortunate that a young boy had come into her charge. Henry's father, Charles Woodstow, had been the companion of his Winchester schooldays, light of heart, impetuous, ardent in his enthusiasm. His own master at eighteen, married at twenty, and dead of a broken neck at twenty-three through trying to train a young stallion with a spirit as surcharged as his own as a hunter in too short a time. His death had led to the death of his young wife through a miscarriage, which had left Henry an orphan at two years of age with an older cousin of Charles Woodstow, Matthew Woodstow, appointed the boy's guardian. A soft, amiable, weak man, Matthew, who for the sake of a quiet life, allowed Amelia to have her own way in most things. Nick was 'uncle' only by courtesy. He did as much as was in his power to make it a genuine role, both for Henry's sake and for the sake of the boy's father.

He remembered then, what Henry had told him of the cousin coming to join the Woodstow household. Whatever her misdeeds had been she was likely to tread a penitential path in Amelia's household. He suspected that Matthew had presented his wife with a ready-made situation – an invitation already given and accepted before Amelia was told of it. Amelia, he was sure, would not receive a young woman fallen from grace with any gladness.

But that, he thought thankfully, was no concern of his.

CHAPTER TWO

Surveying Elswick through the window of the hired chaise as it jolted its way into the village, Elise Hilliard wondered if anything ever happened here. It looked prosperous and picturesque with its single-storeyed thatched and whitewashed cottages, flowers and cabbages elbowing each other for space in the gardens and fishing nets draped over lines or bushes. There was a cluster of mixed housing and one small shop close to the church, and a small green was flanked by a smithy and an inn. She supposed there must be larger properties behind the occasional high wall or the few well-grown trees she had passed, but, all in all, there seemed little promise of variety of interest.

She sighed. It was smaller and quieter even than her expectation. Bath might not be a centre of fashionable life as once it had been, but it still offered a diversity of entertainment by way of concerts, lectures, plays, balls and soirées. She supposed she could live without those for a time, but she would miss the fun of discussing the latest news and town talk with her friends and listening to their light-hearted, quick-witted banter. It looked as though she was in for a season in purgatory.

The hired chaise slowed, turned in between high gates standing invitingly open and travelling over a short, well-kept drive drew to a halt before a neat, plain, but substantial villa with a semi-circular pillared porch and tall windows. The plump middle-aged maid sitting beside her heaved a large sigh of relief.

'Those roads, Miss Elise! Was there ever worse. 'Tis a mercy we've arrived without something breaking. I thought it 'ud be my back.'

'Never mind, Betty. We are safely here and you'll soon be comfortable, I'm sure.'

'If worse don't befall. Sussex is a woeful, backward place, if you ask me,' Betty grumbled darkly, as she heaved herself to her feet and followed her mistress out of the chaise.

Standing on the raked gravel, Elise took her first deep breath of sea air then turned to look at the house. Cousin Matthew, she found, was already coming out from the porch with a wide, welcoming smile. She had not seen him in the seven years since he had left Bath for Elswick, and not surprisingly he looked a little older. His hair was less thick and unruly than she remembered it, and there was grey threading the brown, but otherwise she could see small change in him.

Releasing her from his hug, he held her off and looked her up and down. 'No longer a little girl,' he said 'but a very handsome young lady. Well, well, well, how the years do fly and how good it is to see you again, my dear.'

'And how good you are to have invited me.' And that was true, she thought. She had told him the reason she needed sanctuary and his response had been both warm and immediate, nor was there any hint in his manner now that her visit was not made in quite normal circumstances. She turned to the wife she had not met previously.

So erect did Amelia Woodstow hold herself, she looked taller than she was, an effect contributed to by the narrow last on which she was built and by the exact neatness of everything about her. Acknowledging their introduction, she greeted Elise with funereal restraint, pecking her cheek with an inarticulate murmur rather in the manner of welcoming someone into a house of mourning. Elise felt a lurch of dismay. Never would she have imagined her blithe, easy-going Cousin Matthew choosing such a woman for his wife. And Matthew, she suspected, had confided the reason for her coming to the woman. She, it appeared, did not share her husband's liberal views. Elise could only hope the icy reserve would thaw in time.

Henry had followed closely behind Amelia Woodstow and now stepped forward to make his bow. This young boy, Elise recalled, as she responded with a smile and a curtsy, was another cousin, one of her few remaining relatives and someone else she had not met before. He was, too, the owner of Greenaleigh House and she was as much his guest as Matthew's. The boy stared rather solemnly at her for a moment but then offered a hand and said with cool but careful courtesy, 'Welcome to Greenaleigh, Miss Hilliard.'

'Thank you. I am most happy to be here,' she told him, with the wry reflection that *that* was some way short of the truth.

Little more than a week at Greenaleigh House made her realize that the yardstick by which a schoolgirl had measured an indulgent, occasionally seen older cousin, was different from that used by a young woman of twenty. Cousin Matthew was still a pleasant, easy-going man, but she had come to realize that he indulged himself as much as ever he had once indulged his younger relations, shying from hard decisions, unpleasant situations, dissension. Amelia Woodstow on the other hand had a decided taste for dominance before which Matthew faint-heartedly retreated. It could be neither a comfortable nor a happy marriage, Elise thought. Amelia was too firmly addicted to her own opinion and to the narrow creed of the sect in whose doctrines she had been brought up. Matthew regularly escaped to his books behind his firmly closed study door.

Though nothing was said, Elise was very soon aware that Amelia looked askance at her pretty gowns and thought she should be wearing garments closer to sackcloth and ashes.

An invitation to dine with the Ansteys which included Miss Hilliard, brought Amelia's opinions into more open expression.

'You will wish me to excuse your going, I am sure,' Amelia said,

24

when she told Elise of the invitation.

'Oh, no,' Elise said with surprise. 'I thought when you introduced me to Sir Roland and Lady Anstey after church on Sunday, how very agreeable they both were. Of course, if you and Cousin Matthew do not choose to go. . . .'

'Naturally Mr Woodstow and I shall go,' Amelia said sharply. 'But I cannot think that you have any wish to go about into company. The reason for your coming here – the delicacy of your situation— Can you think it wise to lay yourself open to possible embarrassment? A young woman of any sensibility must surely feel fearful of running such a risk.'

Elise regarded her with smiling calm. 'But what risk can there be? You and Cousin Matthew will not have passed on Bath gossip to anyone, and how else is it likely to be current in Elswick?'

A frown appeared between Amelia's brows. 'There is always the risk that someone with acquaintance in Bath has learned of the reason for your coming here. And surely you feel the need for the greatest discretion on your part? A certain reserve in all you do? Lady Anstey mentions the possibility of *dancing*. *That* you must surely shrink from!'

'To the contrary, I love to dance. The prospect makes me positively wish to go.' She gave the woman a wide smile. 'I appreciate your concern for me, Cousin Amelia, but I think it would arouse the greatest curiosity if I were to refuse all invitations and generally behave as though preparing to enter a nunnery. You would be forever answering questions, which you would very much dislike, I am sure. I truly think it wiser for me to accept my share of the Ansteys' kind invitation.'

Amelia stared at her in fulminating silence, unwilling to accept that she had not carried her point. At last, she said severely, 'We must hope none of us have reason to rue your decision.' Tightly folding her lips, she left the room.

The Ansteys lived in the Manor House. Two hundred years old, added to through the years, but still a long, low, unpretentious building with an air of peaceful permanence. Sir Roland was the local magistrate. He and his wife were a genial pair in their early fifties. They were wealthy but had no children and perhaps for that reason, delighted in surrounding themselves with young guests and gave frequent dancing parties much to the satisfaction of Elswick's younger people.

Sir Roland's small, grey-green eyes twinkled happily as he and Lady Anstey received their guests at the door of their drawing-room. Lady Anstey had been a very pretty girl and still possessed a slim and graceful figure. Both before and after marriage she had lived a blessedly comfortable life, lacking nothing except excitement. It followed naturally, that excitement was the one thing she craved. She did her best with what fell to others by elevating any tale of mishap she heard into a fateful legend which she happily retold prefaced by the words 'Doom, doom, doom!'

She greeted Elise with all the kindness due to a newcomer and took her on a tour of introductions. The drawing-room was comfortably full and looking around, Elise thought she was probably seeing the greater part of Elswick's society. The company did not appear so very different from what was to be found in Bath. There were no extravagances of fashion, of course, and quite a few of the women's gowns were a year or two behind the times. As the only stranger, she was of first interest and very much stared at, but nowhere met with anything other than mild curiosity and pleasant goodwill. With one possible exception. . . .

It seemed to her that the Mr Mariott whom Lady Anstey presently presented to her regarded her with a look of searching attention and some gravity. He shook the hand she offered, exchanged a few politenesses, but made no attempt to extend the conversation beyond the minimum.

Elise sensed his reserve and was certain there had been busy thought behind his dark eyes. Something about her had surprised him, and for that to be so, he must have had a particular expectation.

Could he, by ill-chance, be the one Amelia had foretold might

26

have connections in Bath who had passed on the story of the scandal she had thought to leave behind? He had already been pointed out to her as the major landowner in the neighbourhood, from which she might infer Nicholas Mariott would have considerable influence in the village. If he chose, he could cause her some embarrassment.

She had no intention of worrying about it, but when opportunity offered, she took a long, covert look at him. Her original impression of a moderately tall, well-made man a year or two short of thirty was confirmed. His fine-boned face might even be thought good-looking in an austere way. Dark hair, just short of being called black, matched his dark eyes. Judging by his expression, a degree of gravity was natural to him. Intelligent, she decided, but lacking humour and poor company because of it.

Twice in the course of dinner, Mr Mariott brought himself to her attention again by staring at her. The Ansteys' table comfortably accommodated the twenty-six people now present. Nicholas Mariott was seated on the other side and about three places down from where she was sitting. On both occasions his gaze was sombre and speculative, and on both occasions he withdrew his gaze in a manner suggesting annoyance. As though, Elise thought amused and irritated at the same time, he blamed *her* for having discovered him staring.

A few minutes later, she saw him listening with close attention to the middle-aged woman on his right. He greeted the end of her story with a look of such gleaming acuity accompanied by a spurt of delighted laughter, that Elise's earlier summing up was momentarily shaken. However, on the principle of one swallow not making a summer, she saw no reason to revise her general opinion of him.

Nick had given no thought to the Woodstows' erring cousin from the time he had first heard of her until this evening, but when they were introduced, he realized that Henry's revelation regarding her had sown in his mind some anticipation of the kind of woman she

27

would be. The reality surprised him. She had nothing about her of a flighty Bath Miss who had mistaken her man and her powers of attraction, nor could she be thought a spinster who had failed in a last desperate throw to catch a husband. Whatever lay beneath, her outward seeming was that of a good-looking young woman of no more than nineteen or twenty, quietly self-possessed, with a pleasing voice and an elegant figure. Most men must surely find her attractive. So how had she come to allow herself to fall to ruin with a man unwilling to marry her? Unless. . . . Had she aimed too high? A titled man, perhaps, who refused to be coerced into a plebeian connection where there was only a small fortune to compensate?

Her unmarried state and her flight from Bath taken together told against her. A well-brought-up female took care to avoid indiscreet action that endangered her reputation, and in the ordinary way, any man who found himself – however inadvertently – to have compromised a lady's reputation would be bound in honour to offer her marriage since she had no other hope of retaining her place in society.

Miss Hilliard therefore, presented him with a puzzle, and with no conscious intention of doing so, he had twice found himself staring at her – and each time, to his chagrin, he had been caught doing so. Partly responsible for drawing his attention was that something in her size, shape and colouring woke an old memory. Unwanted. Disturbing.

The Anstey house was blessed with a sizeable central hall which gave ample space for dancing when cleared of furniture and rugs as it was tonight. It was obvious that dancing had quickly passed from being a mere possibility to being positively provided for and several younger guests arrived after dinner to share the pleasure. A musical trio had been recruited from the village and two sets of ten couples were formed for the first dance.

The musicians were amateur but enthusiastic and if there was less refinement in the style of dancing than was to be found in Bath, no one appeared to care. The evening went with a swing and Elise soon realized that the people of Elswick made the most of whatever entertainment there was, cheerfully suffering the inconveniences of ill-kept roads to reach it.

She danced every dance and so did Mr Mariott. He was not, however, among the gentlemen who offered themselves to her as partners.

Captain Robert Penn came to Danesfield on a fine dry day at the end of the third week in August. Presenting his credentials to Nicholas Mariott, he sought permission to survey Danesfield land where it bordered the coast with a view to discovering the most advantageous position for his shore-party to be stationed.

Outwardly, there was some similarity in their appearance, both being lean, dark men of about the same age. Each brought a certain wariness to the meeting but their hopes and aims were not alike. Penn's were directed to obtaining the best he could that would contribute to the success of what he was here to do. Success was an imperative to him. If success could be outstanding and so work towards advancing his career, so much the better.

What Nick looked for was a promise of some understanding in the officer who would be in command of what the naval seamen did in pursuing the purpose of their presence in Elswick. What he hoped to find was some assurance that Penn was not a man who had been brutalized by naval life. Many were. The harsh conditions, ruthless discipline, savage punishments, necessary though they might be, left mercy a long way behind.

When he left, the captain could congratulate himself on having been courteously received, of having had alternatives to his preferences civilly discussed and permission given for a brick-built watch-house to be built on a convenient site. There was no obligation on a landowner to make this last concession, and a refusal would have meant winter under canvas on an exposed coast. Nevertheless there remained some slight sense of dissatisfaction. He had discovered no particular weakness in Nicholas Mariott, or, indeed, any real clue to the man's nature. Probing for some clue to Mariott's personal attitude to the smugglers, whom he must know operated in the locality, he had drawn nothing stronger than a terse agreement to Penn's observation that contraband-running must be considered contrary to the interests of the country as a whole. Had the man any strong opinions, Penn wondered? Or was he one of those who ran with the hare and hunted with the hounds?

He left Nick equally thoughtful. On the whole the captain had made a favourable impression. His uniform had been immaculate, something that could not be said of all naval officers. His approach had been gentlemanly and he had given an impression of being a competent officer, but he had revealed little else.

Not for the first time, Nick was brought up against his awareness of the division between his reason and his instinctive loyalties. Impartiality was not easy. Penn's task was not going to be a simple one, if what was happening elsewhere was any measure of it. It was one reason only volunteers were recruited for Blockade duties. In many places the shore-parties met with virulent hostility, with injury and death as daily threats. It was eleven years since the government had begun a determined effort to put down smuggling: they had been rewarded by some success but it was far from being complete.

Josh Ryland's band was not a large one but they were all Elswick men – Nick's own people for whom he felt a large degree of responsibility. Much depended on how Penn went about his business. If only he could be sure that the man could find some compassion for the difficulties many villagers found in wresting a living from the world around them.

If!

CHAPTER THREE

It had disappointed Elise that in the four weeks she had been at Greenaleigh she had been able to make very little advance into friendship with Henry. She liked the boy and felt a considerable degree of sympathy for him in his rather bleak home life. Yet it seemed to her that though always polite, he kept a distance between them.

With Matthew so often hidden behind his closed study door and Amelia, never overtly unkind, but appearing to look on Henry as an uninteresting lodger in a house she had come to regard as her own, Elise felt his loneliness. It did not surprise her that Henry spent as much time away from Greenaleigh as possible. She found herself following his example. But where, Elise often wondered, as she roamed the lanes and footpaths, did Henry go? From ten until two, five days of the week, he was at his lessons with the Reverend Staunton, but providing he came punctually to table, was clean and neat when he appeared and gave no evidence of having consorted with the village urchins, Amelia showed no concern over his absence.

Surprising herself, Elise had soon found herself enjoying her exploring and delighting in the wide changeable skies, the sharp, clear light and all the moods and colours of the sea that compensated for the flatness of land south of Chichester. September was on its best behaviour and on this mid-month bright Saturday morning she decided to follow to its end the wandering lane, aptly

31

named Long Lane. She had left what she thought was the last of the village houses behind, when she was surprised to have a small, hot hand suddenly thrust into hers. Lost in thought, she had not heard Henry come up behind her.

Falling in beside her, he said, 'Hallo. Would you like to see something special? Something I could show you?'

'I should like it very much.' Elise smiled down at him. 'Where is this special thing?'

'I'm on my way there now. It isn't far.'

What was special to a 9-year-old boy might not appear so to her, Elise realized, but she prepared to appear suitably impressed with whatever it was. The lane led north away from the village towards Chichester and was set between hedges which allowed only an occasional glimpse of what lay on either side when a field gate was passed.

Having made his offer, Henry was now finding it difficult to keep from revealing the nature of his surprise. He shot several side glances at Elise longing for her to press him to tell her, but in the maddening manner of adults, she continued to walk serenely at his side as though seeing something special was an everyday matter to her. 'It's a dog!' he burst out at last. 'And we go through here. It's quicker.' Darting to the side of the lane he thrust open a small gate which gave entry to a weather-stunted copse. Politely, he held the gate open for her.

Elise hesitated. 'Is it all right for me to come with you, Henry? Whose dog is it?'

'He's mine,' Henry said proudly. 'My godfather looks after him for me, but I can come and see him whenever I want and take him out. Bringing someone to see him won't matter at all.'

Fleetingly, as they walked the path between the trees, Elise wondered briefly who Henry's godfather was, but was more interested in the oddness of an arrangement whereby Henry's dog was kept other than at Greenaleigh House. The path suggested the house at its end could only be a cottage, but after a short divergence on to a branch path she found they had entered a

32

substantial stableyard. Elise stopped abruptly, feeling all the awkwardness of an intruder.

'Henry,' she said anxiously, 'who is your godfather?'

At that moment a young groom came out from one of the loose-boxes and seeing them, called, 'Hallo, Master Henry. Come to see Dotty? He's in the tack-room with the master.' He jerked his head towards another door just as a dog's sharp bark sounded from behind it.

'He knows I'm here!' Henry sped away across the setts of the yard towards the door indicated. It opened before he reached it and boy and dog met in ecstatic greeting until Henry tripped and they rolled together on the ground leaving Elise gazing in flushed embarrassment at the man who had followed the dog out into the yard.

Nicholas Mariott was dressed for riding from which he had just returned judging by the dust on his boots. She had met him once or twice at various houses since the Ansteys' dancing-party, but beyond a brief exchange of the usual courtesies they had not spoken. He crossed towards her now, looking as sober as he always seemed whenever she saw him.

'Miss Hilliard . . . good morning.'

'Mr Mariott.' She gave him a stiff little bow, feeling ridiculously embarrassed to have been found here on his property. 'I fear I am trespassing. Henry wished to show me his dog. I did not know. . . .' She left the sentence unfinished.

The boy and the dog's first raptures were over and Henry, on his feet again, was holding the Dalmatian's collar. His glance swung between the two adults as he led the dog towards Elise. 'His name's Dotty,' he said. 'He doesn't shake a paw, though I've tried to teach him.'

Glad to be able to turn from Nicholas Mariott, Elise put out a hand to stroke the broad silky head of the handsome animal. 'I suspect he has too much dignity for that sort of thing. He really is very splendid.'

Henry beamed satisfaction.

'Dotty's just had a long run and could do with a rest before you take him out. He's still young; his bones not yet fully up to his size,' Nick said. 'Perhaps Miss Hilliard and you would like to come into the house for a while and see what my housekeeper can provide by way of refreshments.'

'Oh, no. I mean, no, thank you. I met Henry quite by chance . . . just when I was about to turn back. I really must go.' Elise was aware she was gabbling, but Mr Mariott must not to be allowed to think she was here to pry around his home estate – or worse, that she wanted to thrust herself on his notice. Turning to Henry, she said briskly, 'Thank you for showing me Dotty, Henry. He really is a prince among dogs.'

She turned back as swiftly to Mr Mariott to bid him good day, but before she could speak, he said, 'Pray don't run away, Miss Hilliard. Cannot you stay for a little while?'

Her mind set on the awkwardness of this unwanted meeting, she was not to be persuaded. 'I thank you, but I cannot. I beg you will excuse me. Good day, sir.' Another small bow and she whisked herself around to walk away with brisk certainty.

Nick watched her go with a vexed conviction that Miss Hilliard had snubbed him.

The thoughts of the villagers seeing the watch-house walls rise steadily in the field Nick had provided for the use of the naval shore-party were hidden behind stolidly unrevealing Sussex faces. More visible was the sly pleasure taken by the fishermen among them for the naval men's distaste for the scales and slime that so readily transferred to their hands and clothing in the course of the sporadic searches made of boats returning to harbour. Even more did the fishermen enjoy the navy's total lack of success in finding anything to do with smuggling.

But then Penn hauled in his first prisoner.

'Who?' Nick gazed at his head groom who had given him the news, his astonished question already coloured by laughter.

'Like I said, sir, Saul Wadey.' John Hammond's mouth slipped out of control into a wide grin. 'Caught with the goods. No mistake about it. So they do say.'

'Surely not! Anyone but young Wadey!'

'Most folk do think so. But there was close on a dozen to see him taken. Young Molly's crying herself blind, they being not long wed and her now in the family way.' The groom's expression sobered, asked a question.

'Yes,' Nick said, answering it. 'I'll look into it, John. Have Rahu ready for me in about ten minutes. I'll call on Captain Penn.' He turned towards the house.

Saul Wadey was one of his tenants, therefore it was expected that he should bestir himself on the man's behalf. But *Saul Wadey!* He found himself grinning as Hammond had. A solemn young man, as pious in his way as Amelia Woodstow, but with a simpler mind and a kinder nature. Of all the young men in Elswick, the least likely to have any connection with the smuggling trade. Smuggling. . . . The word sobered him and he swung round.

'John!' The groom came towards him. 'Obviously there has been a run. . . . Were either of the cobs borrowed?'

'No, sir.' The groom's face was suddenly carefully blank.

'You missed out on your brandy this time then?'

Hammond looked uncomfortable. 'No, sir.'

'The brandy was left but no horses were borrowed. Is that it?'

'Yes, sir.'

'I see.' He turned away again.

Indeed, he did see! It took a long moment to control the fierce spurt of revived anger that rose in him. Danesfield working horses had been 'borrowed' for smuggling purposes since his father's time and probably well before that. When a run was made a large number of horses were needed for a short time to ensure speedy dispersal of the goods to inland depots and other destinations. The borrowings were paid for by a gift of brandy or whatever commodity was known, or thought to be, most appreciated by the owners of the horses.

In Elswick, as in other villages, few things remained secret for long. Josh would know that his own practice was to give anything so left to be divided between the two grooms and old Sheldon, his father's coachman, now retired. Josh, it appeared, had decided the men were not to be deprived of their usual windfall because of his rift with their master.

When his anger with Josh after their quarrel in the Sussex Oak had cooled, he had thought – had been certain – there would be a reconciliation. But it had been Josh who had brought about the quarrel and he had left it to Josh to take the first step. The step he had now taken was not towards reconciliation – it was to underline their severance, a mark of contempt.

Well, damn him! Nick thought. If that was what Josh wanted, so be it.

Six of the tents in the field above the harbour were set out in a precise group with the seventh, which had an extension on one side, standing apart. The flaps of both sections of this tent were tied back. A neatly dressed, middle-aged civilian emerged from the extension as Nick rode through the gateway and approached as though ready to take his horse. Penn's personal servant, Nick guessed, and with a smile waved the man aside.

'He's not comfortable with strangers,' he said, as he dismounted and secured Rahu to the gatepost himself.

Penn was visible, at work on a litter of papers spread on a small deal table. A cot bed, a small chest, a document box, a portable cupboard, a second chair and a painted, chequered sailcloth covering on the ground made up the total furnishing and was a long way from comfort. The one item of luxury was a decanter and glasses standing on top of the cupboard. Penn, spruce as ever, rose as Nick entered, produced a careful smile and said, 'Mr Mariott, good day. What can I do for you?'

Against his own mood, Nick tried for a little humour. 'I am here in hope of procuring the release of the most God-fearing, law-abiding seaman you are likely to find in Elswick.'

'I see.' Cool, quiet and unamused.

Waving Nick to take the second chair, as uncompromisingly hard as his own, Penn reseated himself. In the same dry tone as before, he said, 'I must tell you that your law-abiding seaman was taken in possession of contraband goods, which places a doubt upon his claim to be law-abiding. As for his being God-*fearing*, he seemed rather to feel he stood close enough to the Almighty to have the right to his unquestioning support. He called loudly and often on Him to bear witness to his innocence.'

'I doubt if there is a soul in Elswick who would not also bear witness to it.'

'If report is to be believed, there is not a soul between here and Sheerness who would not bear witness to the innocence of every smuggler still at liberty in Kent and Sussex.' Penn's tone was drier still. 'However, lacking the Almighty's personal intervention on Wadey's behalf, I take leave to doubt his innocence.' He neatened the pile of papers immediately in front of him and leaned back as far as his unyielding chair allowed. 'What is your interest in Saul Wadey, Mr Mariott?'

'He is a tenant of mine.'

Nick thought that sufficient explanation, but Penn's brows rose. 'So?'

With generations of landowning Mariotts behind him, he answered with mild surprise, 'Naturally I interest myself in any major difficulties my people face.'

'*Naturally*' and '*my people . . .*' Penn felt the prick of envy at the security expressed in that statement. He said, 'I fear he is unlikely to be paying you rent for a while.'

There was a brief pause and then Nick asked, 'Have you presented him to a magistrate yet?'

'No. But it will be done before the day is out.'

'May I ask the nature of the contraband Wadey was carrying?'

'It was a half-anker of brandy.'

'Nothing more than that? Did he explain it?'

'He said it came up in his nets.'

37

'So he had just come in from fishing. Was the brandy hidden?'

'No.'

'Then you may be sure that what Wadey says is true and if I know anything of the man, given opportunity, he would have taken the brandy to Sir Roland, our magistrate. Wadey's place of worship is a tin tabernacle near Sidlesham. The congregation follow a hell-fire doctrine and he would go to the stake rather than tell a lie, or take to himself as much as a nail that was not his.'

Penn shrugged. 'I accept that you believe what you say, Mr Mariott, but where is there proof of your words?'

There was a flatness in Penn's voice, a hint of impatience, as though he thought that all that was useful had been said. Nick knew his own mood to be unusually volatile and took care to rein back his impatience. With friends in high places in the navy, he was well informed on many counts relating to it. He said carefully, 'Before coming here, may I ask if you had experience of Blockade work, Captain?'

'No. I am lately back from service overseas.'

'Then allow me to make a suggestion. Discover from Wadey where he was fishing and see if you cannot creep up the rest of a string of barrels there. It is a common ploy among the smugglers to sow half-anker barrels attached to a rope weighted to hold them a little below the sea's surface until a convenient time for their recovery. Almost certainly, the one in Wadey's possession had broken from such a string. You may be too late, of course. Even so, most men found in Wadey's predicament walk free because experienced magistrates know what they say is likely to be true. I think you would be wise to give the man the benefit of the doubt.'

Penn did not speak immediately. He sat looking down at the papers on his desk, the muscles in his jaw flexing and unflexing as he considered the probable truth of what Nick had said. And its corollary. Releasing his prisoner did not greatly trouble him, but given Wadey's character and his own ignorance of something that was common knowledge, there would be laughter among the locals. Mariott was giving him opportunity for an early recover. He should be grateful to the man . . . and was not.

Nick watched him with sympathetic understanding. With all to learn, he had come to a difficult task set about with a surfeit of rules and counter-rules issued by the Admiralty, the government, Customs, *et al*. To start with a mistake was not the end of the world, but the laughter of onlookers was hard to bear, particularly for a man of Penn's stamp, which he was beginning to see as unbending. He rose to his feet, said quietly, 'I leave the matter with you, Captain. Good day to you.'

Penn nodded, unable to find grace for more. Nick forgave him for it, but as he was about to step outside the tent, Penn said sharply, 'If you can spare me another moment, Mr Mariott. . . . Joshua Ryland. It appears to be an open secret that he leads your local smugglers. Do you know him?'

'I imagine I know every man in the village, at least by name.'

'Is he one of your tenants?'

'No. He owns his own cottage.'

'So if he runs into any major difficulty you are unlikely to feel the need to interest yourself on his behalf?'

The question was sour. Nick stepped back inside the tent, his eyes suddenly narrowed and black. 'Josh is perfectly capable of taking care of himself.'

Josh, not Ryland. Not even Joshua, Penn noted. 'You know him well then?'

'He was born in this village and so was I. He taught me to row a boat and to sail.'

'And are you one of his customers?'

There could be no mistaking the hostility of that question. Nick felt the dangerous slide of his temper. He said roughly, 'I am no one's customer for smuggled goods. Nor have I been offered any by Josh or anyone else in the village. To save you asking, I will add that I have no share in any smuggling operations, or in the financing of them. I'd be a fool not to know it goes on, but I have been away from Elswick too often and too long to know the who, the what and the where of it.' If that stretched the truth somewhat, be

39

damned to it! He drew breath, said in a quieter tone, 'That is all I have to say, Captain, so if you have no other matter to raise, I will take my leave of you.'

He walked out of the tent to the gate and having unhitched Rahu, rode out by Shore Lane to the southern edge of the village towards the Wadeys' cottage. He recalled his defence of Josh with wry surprise. It had been a spontaneous response to Penn's attempt to goad him. He supposed that, even isolated as the naval men were, some echo could have been caught of the local gossip concerning his friendship with Josh, and possibly a rumour of its disruption, too. But as he had told Penn, Josh could take care of himself. Even so, as he was discovering, old loyalties were not easily set aside.

The Wadeys' cottage was the first of a row of six on the left-hand side of Field Lane. It was a short lane ending at the south wall of the churchyard. All six, single-storeyed cottages belonged to the Danesfield estate, as did the four larger, two-storeyed cottages opposite them. All had been built in the early years of the eighteenth century and each had a small garden before it and a larger one behind. Nick ran an observant eye over them and was satisfied with what he saw. Leaving Rahu, irritated by a second interruption to his exercise, tethered to the nearest strong-looking post, he passed along the rough crazy paving of the path to the cottage door which stood open. Having knocked, he called 'Mrs Wadey' and stepped inside.

Molly Wadey, tear-stained, dishevelled, five months' pregnant and still a month short of her seventeenth birthday, sat on a bench. The arm about her shoulders belonged to the last comforter he might have expected to see here. Nick was unaware that, recognizing Miss Hilliard, he scowled.

Miss Hilliard, on the other hand, was very much aware of it.

CHAPTER FOUR

Sheer fright at the appearance of the man who owned her home and who could toss her out into the street at a moment's notice dried Molly Wadey's tears. Floundering to her feet she made a travesty of a curtsy, her eyes huge with apprehension.

With a hasty nod in Miss Hilliard's direction, Nick smiled at the distraught young wife and said gently, 'Sit down, Mrs Wadey, please. I bring you good news, so take heart. Before too long I think you may look to see your husband home. Captain Penn may need to have Saul take him to the fishing grounds where he brought up the brandy in his nets, but, depending on the tide, it should be no more than an hour or two before he is home with you.'

The result of this comforting speech was Molly's collapse into deep sobbing tears of relief.

Elise had been hoping to escape, but now she drew the girl down on to the bench from which they had risen, murmuring small encouragements towards calmness.

Helpless before young Molly's tears, Nick found reason to be grateful for Miss Hilliard's presence after all.

Molly's sobs abating, she hiccupped her way to further reassurance, asking, 'He really will come home? Because he never would go for a smuggler, sir. He never would.'

Nick reaffirmed his prediction of Saul's return and she said with shy dignity, 'Then thank you kindly for coming to tell me.'

Preparing to depart, Elise gave her a final, encouraging hug. 'You should rest now after so much upset. Then I expect you will want to prepare a meal for your husband. He's sure to be hungry when he comes.' Even if he was not, it would serve to stop her counting the minutes and building up her fears again. She turned to the door.

Mr Mariott turned with her. 'Miss Hilliard, if you are going back to Greenaleigh, it will be my pleasure to escort you.'

She accepted without demur since it would be churlish to do otherwise and they left with Molly curtsying gratefully in the doorway.

Walking down the path, Nick remembered Rahu, who, being in no mood to be walked homeward when he was wanting a good run, would make an awkward third. As though to emphasize the point, Rahu neighed shrill indignation when they passed where he was tethered. Nick put his faith in Miss Hilliard not knowing the horse was his and was thankful he had not left the animal immediately outside the Wadey cottage.

When they were some distance past the horse, he said, 'We pass the smithy. If you will bear with me a moment, I need to step in for a moment to see Tallack.'

She said quickly: too quickly, perhaps, 'You must not allow me to keep you from your own purposes, Mr Mariott. It is not at all necessary for you to walk me back to Greenaleigh. I shall simply be returning as I came, alone.'

'I am aware. But do not, I beg, make it a reason to escape my company.' Having made up his mind to free his conscience of its sense of guilt where Miss Hilliard was concerned, he preferred to get it done as soon as possible.

Elise said no more and they walked the short distance to the turning into the High Street in reasonable amity, though it occurred to Nick with some wryness that if Miss Hilliard was anxious to find a husband, *he* was not under consideration. There were no sideways glances, no fluttering eyelashes. That he was the most eligible *parti* in Elswick had been thrust on him since his return from his travels and he thought it unlikely that no one would have informed her of the fact. Miss Hilliard evidently found nothing in it to interest her.

The smithy with its short row of stables embraced by a paddock, occupied a corner where Church Lane crossed the High Street. Elise chose to remain at the rail of the paddock to watch its sole occupant, a pretty little dapple pony who came up to her smartly in the hope of a carrot or apple.

Inside the smithy, Nick asked John Tallack, the smith, to collect Rahu and stable him until he came again or sent for him.

'Fetch him yourself, John, if you will. Your lad would never manage him. He's not in the best of tempers,' he warned.

Tallack, 54 years old and well-acquainted with both horse and owner, said with a sigh, 'When is he ever? Peevish even at his best. Can't think why you want such an unaccountable beast. A Turk by breed and a Turk by nature.' It was an old plaint and Nick merely smiled and said, 'Thanks, John.'

Returning to Miss Hilliard, he said after a moment, 'It was unexpected to find you consoling Molly Wadey. How did you learn she was in trouble?'

'Henry told me the story and that everyone was laughing because Saul Wadey was so improbable a smuggler. He also said Saul had not been long married and his wife was very distressed. I thought there might be something I could do for her.'

'It was good of you to take the trouble.'

She gave him a fleeting amused glance and he realized that his reaction when he had first seen her had not gone unnoticed. He hurried on, 'How did Henry know?'

'I think your head groom, Hammond, told him.'

'I see. Yes. It was Hammond who told me. Molly is a cousin of his. Several times removed, but still family. Henry came early to see Dotty on his way to his lessons with the vicar. I didn't see him because I was engaged with my bailiff at the time.'

'Seeing Dotty was hardly on Henry's way to the vicarage,' Elise said, smiling.

43

'When Henry wants to see Dotty, Danesfield is "on his way".'

They had slowed their steps to a halt as they reached the gates of Greenaleigh. His attention caught by the attraction of her smile, Nick stood silent for a moment, then, on an impulse, he put out a hand. 'May I say we are now friends, Miss Hilliard?'

Her smile faded and she gave him a long, gravely considering look. 'Perhaps friendly acquaintance would be more accurate. Friendship takes time, I think. Time to put down roots.' But she took his hand and her smile returned to soften the austerity of her words.

He opened one leaf of the gates and she walked through. When he did not follow, she turned to ask,'Will you not come in?'

'I think not. Please say all that is proper to your cousins for me.'

She nodded, bade him goodbye and walked on.

He stood watching until she reached the house, but she did not turn. For a young woman of no more than twenty years she had a formidable self-command and a somewhat severe discriminatory sense. Or was that reserved for use only against himself?

He could remember no occasion in their brief acquaintance when she had left him feeling pleased with himself.

Following Elise's introduction to Dotty, Henry's reserve towards her melted away. Quite often now, he joined her on afternoon walks, both with and without his dog. He chattered happily at her side or skipped along the tide-line on the shore looking for treasure. He was her guide to the hinterland of Elswick, so that she soon had a very good idea where most of the lanes and tracks led and what else lay between Elswick, Chichester and Selsey. She learned, too, that Henry had conceived a strong admiration for Captain Penn out of that unfailing lure for small boys, a handsome uniform.

In common with the rest of Elswick, though Elise had seen him in church, she had yet to meet Captain Penn, but she was willing to agree with Henry that, yes, the captain looked very fine in his naval rig, and, yes, she was sure the navy offered a man a career worth considering.

44

Henry had spent another Saturday morning roaming far and wide with Dotty before returning him to Danesfield, but still had energy to happily devote the afternoon to escorting Elise on one more ramble around the environs of Elswick.

They were walking one of the few remaining and, to Elise, unexplored tracks. This, lying between Danesfield and the village, led out of Long Lane across Mariott land towards the sea. One of the things that had surprised and delighted her about Sussex was the number of solitary cottages tucked away in odd corners among fields, or in woods and hollows, their occupants quite content, it seemed, with a lack of immediate neighbours. The one they now came to, brought her to an admiring halt.

'Oh, what a pretty cottage!'

It stood in a slight hollow near the sea, sheltered on the land side by some low trees mostly thorn though a few twisted apple trees showed here and there. Tile-hung, lattice-windowed, it was a typical Sussex cottage of the better sort. Draped with late roses showing richly cream against the rosy brick and tile, the neat garden around it still surprisingly colourful.

Unconcerned with aesthetics, Henry was hanging over the gate now. 'My friend lives here,' he announced, in a pleased and proprietary way.

Elise thought she knew all Henry's few friends: his godfather, his dog, and – she hoped – now herself. But who else? No children came to Greenaleigh House.

Henry gave a joyful shout. 'He's here! See! Beyond those trees there.' He pointed out the direction.

Looking for a child, Elise could see no one until some suggestion of movement at a higher level drew her attention. Indistinctly through the screening leaves and branches, she saw not a child but a man.

'Come and meet him.' Without waiting for agreement, Henry darted through the gate and pelted down the path. A little uncertainly, Elise followed.

The sound of Henry's flying feet on the random paving had

drawn the man's notice and he came to meet them, greeting Henry with a playful thump on the shoulder.

'This is Josh,' Henry said with the same pride with which he had introduced Dotty to her. 'And this is my cousin, Miss Hilliard,' he told Josh, with a not too noticeable diminution of that pride.

Though Henry had omitted his friend's surname, Elise had no doubt that this was Joshua Ryland who, it was whispered, was the leader of Elswick's smugglers.

'I'm happy to meet you, Miss Hilliard,' Josh said, perfectly at ease.

Looking up at him, Elise met a vividly blue smiling gaze and was somehow compelled to smile back. She held out her hand. 'And I you, Mr Ryland.'

And she should not be, she thought a moment too late. If rumour was to be believed, this was a man who acted in defiance of the law and was likely to end in jail or worse. He was the chief reason Captain Penn and twenty or so naval men were stationed here in Elswick. But there was something decidedly attractive about this large, ruggedly good-looking man with an expression that seemed to live on the edge of amusement.

'Will you come in and meet my wife? Henry is very partial to her blackberry cordial.'

She should decline, whisk Henry away and deliver a careful sermon on the dangers of evil companions. Instead, she accepted, entered through the open door of the house and was introduced to a neatly dressed, comely woman, whom Josh called Prue, and who was as serene as Josh in doing the honours of her house.

Offered a choice between blackberry cordial and what Josh described with an extra twinkle as a 'very good madeira wine', Elise joined with Henry and chose blackberry cordial. They stayed half an hour, their host and hostess sitting with them. There was no shortage of conversation and thinking about it afterwards, she realized there had been a lot of laughter, particularly on Henry's part. And that, she decided, was worth whatever rules she had broken. How, though, she wondered, did Henry reconcile his lionizing of two men so diametrically opposed in their purposes as Josh Ryland and Captain Penn?

Among the impressions Elise carried away with her, one of the strongest was the pleasure and the pride the seaman took in his family, from his wife to the youngest of his three sons, Timothy, aged five, who had returned from the dame-school while they were there.

There had been just one moment of tension when Prue had left the room to refill the jug of cordial and Henry had asked, 'Josh, when are you going to be friends with Uncle Nick again?'

Elise had seen something flash into the blue eyes, had seen the muscles of the deeply tanned face stiffen. But the eyes were hidden, the face relaxed and Josh said, 'Well, we'll have to see, young Henry.' Brief as the passage had been, something had emanated from the seaman that disturbed her.

Henry was thoughtful on the way back to Greenaleigh House, but it was not the quarrel between his godfather and his friend that was on his mind. Before long he asked, 'You liked Josh, didn't you?'

When Elise agreed that she had, he went on, 'Do you think – will you have to tell Aunt Amelia we saw him and went into his house?'

It was an illuminating question and one that made Elise pause before she answered it. Even more was this an opportunity to point to the demerits of deception. Yet in the end, all she said was, 'I see no need. It would not interest her particularly, I think.' And that, surely, was to compound all her lapses today.

Henry heaved a satisfied sigh. 'You *are* a right one, aren't you, Miss Hilliard.'

She looked down at him with a smile. 'Since we seem to have become fellow conspirators, so to speak, I think it's time you called me Cousin Elise, don't you?'

Henry nodded vigorously. 'And will you come with me to see Josh again?'

And *that*, Elise thought, seeking a cautious answer, was what

47

came of deviating from the path of virtue. . . .

The late September day promised to be fair as Nick turned Rahu out of the stableyard on to the track leading into the writhen copse. It was very little past dawn. The sky above the Danesfield stables showed palest green flowing into clear unblemished blue, but as he reached the trees the sun was laying its first wash of gold over all.

Where the track joined the main path he turned left away from Long Lane and towards the sea intending to give Rahu a good run along the coastal path. But where the copse ended he reined in, remaining just inside its cover. Early as the hour was he did not have it to himself. On the far side of the half-acre field before him, where the land dropped a few feet into the sea, caught in the strengthening brilliance of the rising sun and the sea's jubilant reflection of it, was the figure of a woman . . . a girl, perhaps. Not recognizable, a figure of myth and faery, nebulous in the splendour of light. As he watched, she raised widespread arms as though to embrace the glory of sea and sky and morning.

Nick set the Turk moving again and, as he did so, the figure dropped her arms, turned and stood as though – seeing him – she waited. Still made nebulous in outline by the light, it was only when he was quite near could he be sure of her identity: Miss Hilliard. *Who else?* he thought, unsurprised. He knew the maidens and young wives of Elswick well enough to know how unlikely it was that any among them should be here at this hour greeting the golden dayspring like a votary of Apollo. But anything might be expected of this paradoxical stranger who had come among them.

If she suspected he had witnessed that moment of joyous worship there was no trace of embarrassment in the face she turned up to him. Her expression showed only what he supposed was the usual look with which she met those she designated 'friendly acquaintance'. And he, he surmised, was on probation even for that degree of acceptance.

He said prosaically, 'Good morning. You're abroad very early.'

'Yes. As you are, sir.'

'Oh, we farmers, you know . . . up with the lark.'

Her glance flickered over his horse and she smiled. 'A very handsomely mounted farmer.'

'Yes. But I regret to say Rahu's manners do not always match his appearance, which is the reason I must ask you to excuse my failure to dismount.'

'Rahu? I cannot place the name.'

'It is Indian. The name of a Hindu demon who constantly pursues the sun and moon and sometimes catches one or the other causing an eclipse. I read the legend at about the time I acquired this disputatious animal and the name seemed appropriate.'

He saw the gleam of mischief slide into the very handsome pair of grey eyes looking up at him and braced himself.

'Fleet enough to catch the sun and moon, wicked enough to plunge the world into darkness. . . . What does it take to master the demon? Great good or a greater wickedness? And which are you employing, Mr Mariott?'

She laughed up at him and he cursed Rahu's early morning intractability and the lack of anywhere nearby to which he could be tied. Perched in the saddle above her, he felt at a disadvantage and his answer was shorter and sharper than he intended. 'I leave it to you to judge, Miss Hilliard. Whichever you think comes more naturally to my hand.'

Abruptly, amusement leached out of her expression. A pause, and then she said, 'Oh, I leave judgements to others to make. And on that we part, sir. I to go to my breakfast and you to enjoy your ride.'

She was gone, skirting the horse and walking towards the copse along the path by which he had left it.

Holding his fidgeting mount on a tight rein, Nick turned in the saddle to watch her but she did not look back. His mood and his pleasure in the morning were spoiled: spoiled by his unfortunate use of the word *judge* and her readiness to pick it up and use it against him, making sure what she said struck home with her *And on that we part, sir.* Her opinion of him appeared to be fixed on an immovable low and was not going to be easily raised.

And the most damnable thing about it was each time they met he was more aware of her charm.

Once sure she was hidden by the trees of the copse, Elise *did* look back. By then Nicholas Mariott was turning Rahu in a northerly direction along the coastal track, horse and rider an elegant outline against a golden sea.

Elegant, she thought. Yes, that accurately described both man and horse. An elegance of bone complemented by muscle and flesh that had no superfluity. Hatless, coatless, his white shirt unbuttoned at the neck despite the early morning cool, Nicholas Mariott and Rahu together had appeared at one with the day's beauty. Had he known it? No, she absolved him of vanity. But his dark eyes had searched her face as though he sought there some reflection of a particular response from her. It had seemed to her that he had expected – wanted? – *something*.

And then when he had offered her the opening for her remark about judgements, she had snatched at it. It had been less than kind. He had already attempted amend in that direction. Too late, she had seen that her following remark, could be linked with it, adding pith and point.

Well, she told herself, she owed Nicholas Mariott no kindness, though her lack of generosity was to be regretted.

CHAPTER FIVE

It had never occurred to Lady Anstey that when at last adventure found her it might prove to be disagreeable.

The lane on which the Manor House and the Sussex Oak both stood ran north to join the road that ran between Selsey and Chichester and where it ceased to be Elswick's High Street was known as Crooked Lane. Northward, the only three other dwellings were the Manor Farmhouse and two cottages occupied by the farmer's cowman and his man-of-all-work. These three lay slightly off the lane on a short bramble-grown cart-track named The Scratchings. It led nowhere except to a long derelict cottage and was little used apart from traffic to and from the farm.

Lady Anstey had walked to the farmhouse by way of a footpath leading out the manor gardens across a field to enquire after the farmer's youngest daughter who was ill of a recurrent bronchial complaint. A sharp shower of rain during the night had left the path muddier than she had anticipated and by the time she reached the farm she had already decided to return by the slightly longer route of The Scratchings and the lane. This was the way she started back.

Toby Wannacott was Elswick's simpleton. He was a large youth barely 16 years old, much given to wandering, but willing and able to perform tasks that required no more than brute strength and a short span of concentration. Chance brought him level with the inn where Tom Forbes, for once in funds, was sitting in a half-fuddled state under the wind-stunted oak tree outside the inn. Calling out to the boy, Tom offered him a drink. Unintended mischief lay in it because what he gave Toby was undiluted naval rum.

Treats rarely came Toby's way and he gratefully drank down what he was given without pausing to discover its nature. With no purpose in mind, he then ambled on, and turned into The Scratchings. By then, he was in an a state of euphoria, a king among men. Lately, his overgrown body had been subject to strange urges of which he had little understanding. Now, however, when he saw coming towards him, a pretty female shape it seemed to his muddled mind to have direct connection with those urges and his present state of well-being. It is doubtful that Toby would have recognized the squire's wife at any time. The fashion was for large hats, too, and Lady Anstey's was broad-brimmed and face-concealing. Coming up with her, Toby did what he felt impelled to do and putting his arms about her drew her into a hard embrace.

Struggling as fiercely as she could against this altogether astonishing assault, when she was able to draw sufficient breath, Lady Anstey screamed.

The struggle, the scream and the strangely provocative feeling of a soft female body in his arms, all added to Toby's excitement. His face found its way under Lady Anstey's hat, his wet lips nuzzling and questing like those of a blind puppy. She screamed again and found deliverance in the moment before she fainted.

Soon after coming to Elswick, Captain Penn had explored The Scratchings to its end, but aware that there had been a recent smuggling run, he had chosen to revisit it today to cover the possibility of the derelict cottage being used as a temporary store. He had found it disappointingly unchanged, no hint that its tumbledown cob walls supporting the rotting remains of a thatch roof had ever been used to hide anything since the last occupants departed.

Riding slowly away from the ruin, Penn was sour with frustration engendered by the difficulty of finding hard evidence against even the one man whose name he had heard whispered in connection with the so-called 'trade' – the key man, the leader, if there was any truth in it. Gossip might give him a name, but without being able to catch the man in possession of contraband, he could make no move against him except for one alternative and that was to find two men of standing to swear to the man's involvement in smuggling. And here in Elswick he had found nothing so far to encourage him to hope for such co-operation.

He was watching where his horse was putting his feet on the rough track when he heard the scream and looking up, saw at a small distance a slight female shape struggling in the arms of an ill-dressed hobbledehoy. He came smartly up to the pair, swung to the ground and hauled the youth off his prey as Lady Anstey slid limply to earth. A blow to the jaw sent Toby reeling and one glance at the prostrate woman told the captain she was no rustic maiden but a well-dressed older woman of some substance. He looked towards Toby to see if further trouble could be expected from his direction, but all Toby's fires had been effectually doused and the sight of the captain's uniform terrified him. As soon as he had gathered half his feeble wits together, he howled aloud and took to his heels at a stumbling run.

He was fortunate that Penn's first concern was for the woman on the ground rather than inflicting further punishment on her attacker. Lady Anstey was showing signs of recovery and, kneeling down beside her, Penn supported her into a sitting position. After a few dazed moments, she was able to tell him who she was and what little else she could.

'It was Toby Wannacott,' she said with a shiver of distaste. 'A poor fool but always believed harmless.'

'In need of thrashing to curb his ardours, ma'am.'

She shook her head in helpless bewilderment, badly shaken and close to tears. 'So big, but no more than fifteen or sixteen. And he had been drinking.'

'Neither good excuses.'

53

When she showed signs of having better control of herself, he helped her to her feet. 'If there was anywhere to leave you, Lady Anstey, I would go to fetch a conveyance—'

'Oh, no! Don't leave me!' Her ladyship threw a frightened glance around as though Toby might leap out of a hedge again at any moment.

'Your own house is as near as any. Do you think you can walk to it with my help?'

'Indeed, I must!' With a small show of returning spirit, she gave him something resembling a smile.

Penn gathered up her hat from the ground and leading his horse, set out with her on a slow journey to the manor. There he saw her into the care of her housekeeper and maid and having given them an outline of her ladyship's unpleasant experience – Sir Roland being absent from the house – he took his leave.

Sir Roland arrived at Danesfield two or three hours later.

Nick made his visitor comfortable beside the fire with a glass of his favourite toddy by his side and waited patiently through a rambling lamentation for the mediocre quality of the harvest, the uncertain weather and the approach of winter, to discover Sir Roland's reason for calling.

Following a silence during which he stared frowningly at the fire, the squire said abruptly, 'Roof's nearly complete on that watch-house they're building.'

'Yes. Penn and his men will be glad to get into it, I should think.'

'Awkward!' the squire said obscurely.

Nick waited for enlightenment and when it did not come, prompted, 'In, what way awkward?'

'Oh, not the watch-house. Lady Anstey. You heard about that unfortunate business with the Wannacotts' mooncalf this morning?'

'No. I've been in Chichester most of the day. Returned about half an hour ago.'

Sir Roland told him what had happened. 'Grateful to him, naturally. On my way to say so now. Thing is, Julia says we will have to ask the man to dine with us, or something of that sort. Feels we can do no less. But as I said, it's deuced awkward.'

He shot Nick a challenging look. 'If you don't know, you've no doubt guessed where I get my brandy. And Julia can't wait to show off the French lace on her newest gown.' His voice gathered a hint of resentment. 'You were thick as thieves with Josh Ryland at one time, yet I've heard you don't buy run goods. Your father did. And his father before him. Bit of a puritan, ain't you, Nick?'

With a shrug of his shoulders, Nick said, 'It was never a conscious decision not to buy contraband. And Josh has not asked me to. Why should he? My father held the reins here until the last month or two before his death and he left Danesfield with a full cellar.'

'Have you thought that letting the navy build on your land won't have improved your popularity with the villagers? *Or* with some of the rest of us.'

'It's not a point I have given much thought to. Penn and his men would be here in our midst whether I let the navy build or not. It seemed pointless to be obstructive.'

'No. Well, it's no business of mine and it wasn't what I came to say. The thing is . . . Penn. What do I do? Invite the man to my house and offer him contraband brandy? He knows I'm a magistrate.' He saw Nick's quizzical expression. 'Yes. Should have thought of that before. But smuggling's been a way of life in Elswick longer than anyone remembers, as it has been for almost any village along the Sussex coast, come to that. Kept the county alive. But you've met Penn. What like is he?'

'If you mean is he a gentleman, yes, he is. But he's here to do a job and he means to do it. He's unlikely to turn a blind eye to anything that goes on in Elswick.' He was surprised to discover how certain he was of that.

'He made a bit of a fool of himself with Saul Wadey.'

'It's not a mistake he'll repeat.'

'Hmm. Well, it seems I shall have to let Julia have her way and invite the man to dine. Hope he don't ask to look in my cellar. It will mean treading the straight and narrow in future. Damn shame, really, Ryland brings in a fine line of goods. Have to choose who else to invite with care. I take it you'll be prepared to come?' He emptied his glass when Nick nodded and heaved himself to his feet. 'Never have been sure that the line between right and wrong is all that straight. Always thought there was a deal of good in many men labelled bad and more than enough of bad in men who pass for good!'

And that, Nick thought, escorting Sir Roland to the door of the house, was what made him a generous and compassionate man and an understanding magistrate.

As for himself, he was less sure than ever of precisely where he stood. He had not bought run-goods for the reasons he had given Sir Roland, but in the fourteen months since his father's death he had winked at the use of his working horses and at the brandy left in payment. Giving it to the men who had the grooming of the horses could be seen as an easy way out, though he had never really thought about it. But it left him in no position to judge anyone else.

The guests the Ansteys selected to meet Captain Penn were chosen from among those who might be considered 'safe' and were not great in number. Amelia Woodstow could be depended to look favourably on the reason for the captain's presence in Elswick and Matthew would take the line of least resistance; Elise was naturally included in their invitation. The Reverend Staunton, unlike the vicar of Selsey who was an ardent supporter of his local smugglers, was regarded as neutral and Mary would never be unkind. The company was completed by Harrison Colbrooke, a retired diplomat, and his wife Sylvia.

Sir Roland had persuaded his wife out of wearing the gown adorned with smuggled lace and dinner was got through with nothing worse than an unfortunately loud-voiced observation from Amelia that 'It is past time for the villainous business of smuggling to be ended. Those who buy smuggled goods are much to blame and should receive some share of the punishment.'

When the gentlemen rejoined the ladies in the drawing-room soon after dinner, Penn chose the most attractive option he could see and, with permission, took a chair at Elise's side. With a wry smile, he asked, 'Do you share Mrs Woodstow's opinion regarding the culpability of those who buy contraband, Miss Hilliard?'

She gave him a quizzical look. 'It seems reasonable to suppose that if the seller of illegal goods is doing wrong then the knowing buyer must also be doing so. But as a mere visitor to Sussex I know too little about what goes on to hold strong views. My cousin lives here and is, perhaps, better informed.'

He suspected she was warning him away from the subject and sensibly, he left it. 'And do you stay here long?'

'Until Christmas. After that, I'm not sure.'

'And then you go where? Someone told me you came here from Bath.'

'Yes. But as to my return there, I have not yet decided.'

He looked at her with interest. It was unusual for so young a woman to decide her own comings and goings. He wondered what her circumstances were. Her long-sleeved gown, pale violet in colour and of a kind of silky gauze, was fashionable and showed a cut and finish superior to most of the other women's gowns. An attractive young woman, too, and perfectly at ease. With a sister married to a gentleman with a small estate on the edge of Bath, Penn thought it might be worthwhile to enquire of that incorrigible gossip what, if anything, she knew of Miss Hilliard.

Penn had done his dutiful part as a young lieutenant in making up numbers at the tables of various captains when they entertained and in partnering spare ladies at balls in governmental houses. He knew how to talk interestingly of the places to which duty had taken him, of sights seen and adventures encountered without making a parade of his own doings. Elise was sorry when he was drawn away by their hostess to answer a question for Mr Colbrooke. Almost immediately his place was taken by Nicholas

Mariott.

From across the room, Nick had seen the smiling welcome she had given the captain and their easy exchanges afterwards. Why, he wondered, did he find it so difficult to put their acquaintance on an equally comfortable, social footing. He had put himself in the wrong at the beginning, but he had tried to redress the matter since. That Miss Hilliard was not easily appeased he had learned at their last meeting. But Elswick was too small a place for quarrels to pass unremarked and he meant to try again to bridge the gap between them. He hoped to at least bring them to a point where they could meet without noticeable unfriendliness.

Which made his opening remark all the more unfortunate. 'All the ladies love a uniform,' he said. And instantly regretted his clumsiness.

'Which is no compliment to our intelligence, Mr Mariott.' There was no hint of reproof in her tone but the words were enough.

'I beg your pardon. I spoke without thought.'

'The unvarnished truth? Well, I do not mean to quarrel with you.' She looked up at him and laughed at his expression. 'No, no. I mean it. Do sit down. Captain Penn has put me in good humour and you may reap the benefit.'

He sat down rather abruptly. 'May I ask what you talked about? I might profit from following his example.'

Her eyebrows flicked up in a way he was beginning to recognize, but she said equably, 'Oh, mostly about his tours of duty in faraway places. I have heard that you spent several years abroad – five was it? – and returned to Elswick little more than eighteen months ago. I envy you gentlemen your freedom to travel abroad.'

'There can be considerable discomfort attached to some journeys.' She had given him an opening and he fell easily into illustrating the point and went on to speak more generally about his travels through Italy, Greece and Albania until struck by the thought that she might think he was entering into competition with Penn, he came to a sudden halt.

'Well, that journey ended suddenly, didn't it?' Her smile teased him and he was again conscious of her charm. When he did not answer immediately, she dropped another question into the silence.

'What do you think was your greatest gain from your travels?'

The ease with which she ruffled his feelings gave him a sudden, perverse desire to flutter hers and, grimly humorous, he said. 'To shoot to kill.'

She should have looked at least a little shaken . . . perhaps exclaimed and shrunk from him . . . but Miss Hilliard exhibited neither of these more usual feminine responses. Her gaze did not waver from his and if the moment before she answered lengthened a little, it was with no more than cool interest that she asked, 'And *did* you kill someone?'

What, he wondered did it take to break her calm? He held her gaze and with stubborn bleakness, told her, 'Yes.' But then, relenting a little, added, 'It was preferable to accepting my own death.'

'Who was so eager for it?'

'An Albanian bandit. Three ponies and the possibility of some gold was the prize anticipated. The odds were in his favour. He was accompanied by two friends. Against them, there was myself and my servant.'

'What happened?'

'The leader made his intention too plain. My own weapon was more modern than his and I was able to fire first. My servant managed to wing another. He, with the third man decamped at once.'

'How did you feel when you realized that the man left behind was dead?'

'Relieved.'

'How old were you?'

'Twenty-five.'

'What happened then?'

'There was nothing we could do for the shot man and we had no means of burying him. We closed his eyes, straightened his limbs and hoped his friends would return to claim him. But not too soon. Paolo, being Italian and a Catholic, made a sign of the cross and muttered what might have been a prayer for his soul. My own prayer was for a safe return to civilization.'

'What a very practical man you are, Mr Mariott.' She slanted an unreadable smile at him.

'And what a very imperturbable young lady *you* are, Miss Hilliard.'

'Like your Albanian bandit, you signalled your intention too plainly.'

Game, set, and match. . . . Miss Hilliard was irritatingly acute.

Later, he realized that in an odd sort of way he had enjoyed the exchange with her. She was refreshingly different; attracted without appearing to make any conscious effort to do so.

But was that due to her skill rather than a lack of artifice? The worm of doubt refused to be entirely suppressed.

CHAPTER SIX

By the end of October, the watch-house was ready for occupation, the tents were struck and the shore-party moved in.

Built to Admiralty specifications, two-storeyed, its forty-eight feet by twenty-eight, had to accommodate twenty naval ratings, three midshipmen, a cook, captain and the captain's servant. It was furnished as basically as it was designed, with hammocks for the seamen and a cot for the officer, but still offered more comfort and better protection than tents provided.

The weather was growing more unsettled with increasingly blustery winds driving squalls of heavy rain before them and whipping the sea into spume-laden waves. The men on watch duty at night – never less than five, spread evenly across a mile of coast, were wholly without shelter. Nor could they relax their vigilance because one or other of the four officers patrolled the line at regular intervals.

The most easterly of the three inlets in the coast close to Elswick, was the shallowest being nothing more than a small incurve with a narrow strip of sand at low tide. Bordered by Danesfield land, it was known as The Bend and having no direct access from the village, was rarely used. One night, the look-out stationed nearby, went down to the narrow strip of beach to find a sheltered corner in which to relieve himself. On his return, stepping past the high-tide line, where the thin, uncertain grass of the headland began, he fell into a concealed hole deep enough to give him an unpleasant shaking. Recovering, he took what stock he could in the darkness, and discovered that the hole was roughly four feet square overall and lined with thick wooden planks. Over this had been laid a kind of wooden tray filled with earth and sand into which grass had grown or been planted. The seaman had done a short spell of Blockade duty at Cuckmere and recognized it as a stowhole constructed to hold contraband for collection at a convenient time. This one was old, empty and rotted, but the possibility was that there might be others of later construction.

Following the sentinel's report, careful search of the area was made. Several other holes were found but they were as old and empty as the first. More interesting was the narrow footpath, little more than a small animal track, leading from The Bend to a solitary cottage of the larger sort. . . .

Soon after midday, news was flying through the village that Josh's cottage had been searched. Giles Ryland, 11 years old, had returned from school for his dinner, to find his mother in a disordered house, weeping over a shattered lamp which had sent a dark spread of oil across a cherished rug and his younger brother, Timothy, aged five, tear-stained and frightened. His mother's distress was such that Giles, both puzzled and troubled, called in the nearest female with whom his mother was friendly. It was this woman's husband, who set more detailed news on its way.

Beginning with an audience of four at the Sussex Oak, he told them with relish, 'Trouble in store. . . . When they raided Josh's place, it wasn't only damage to the household traps they done, they mishandled his Prue and scared the youngest boy half out of his wits. Josh and his eldest'll be back on the evening tide. Then we'll see.'

The search of Josh's lugger, when it came into harbour was oddly perfunctory. Josh, still on deck, eyed the three Elswick men so obviously waiting for him and sensed that news waited with them. Sensed, too, that he would not welcome it.

Nor did he. He said nothing when they told him what had

happened, but he turned his face in the direction of his home as though he could see across the distance to look through its walls. With no more than a nod for his informers, he put them aside and strode away, but his expression told them all that they had waited to see.

The distance between Josh's cottage and the watch-house was not great. Josh came to it little more than an hour after going to his home. Sweeping out of his way the seaman who tried to intercept him at the door, he demanded to see the captain.

The commotion that followed brought Penn to the door of his room. In the momentary stillness as the men looked to their captain for direction, Josh decided the matter for them all. Shaking off those attempting to hold him, he walked past the Penn as though invited, saying, 'Shut the door, Captain. You won't want your men to hear what I have to say.'

Penn shut the door, strode to his desk, turned, and said with cold ferocity, 'Don't take that tone with me, Ryland.'

'What tone I take I'm free to choose. My soul's my own, thank God!' Josh told him grimly.

Penn drew breath as though long deprived. 'Your soul won't remain your own for long after you're caught. And you will be! You are a known smuggler. A thief of the revenues of your country. If you escape hanging, it will be more than you deserve.'

'All to be proved, Captain. But we'll see, won't we? And whatever I am, I have never needed to misuse women, frighten small children and break up their home.'

As bad as that! Penn thought irritably. There was something about Ryland that told him he was not exaggerating. Midshipman Surtees had reported that the Irishman, Johnston, had been drinking and had been heavy handed when the man's cottage was searched.

'Johnston doesn't like these people,' Surtees had said. 'To his mind, they're too quiet. Secretive. He doesn't like their ways. And hates their religion . . . our religion.'

63

Surtees was a slim youth, not yet seventeen: Johnston,a burly thirty something, an uncouth rebel of a man who drank too much. Unfair to expect the first to control the second, but midshipmen had to learn to use their authority and he himself had to use what men he had. The Blockade was not popular in the service and the Admiralty was having to go further and further afield to find recruits for it . . . Newcastle, Plymouth, Cork. . . . Men who, perhaps, had never been to sea and whose only virtue was that they were not pressed men.

Penn, for some reason he could not have explained, was unwilling to believe that Ryland was less of a barbarian than the average peasant. Contemptuously, he said, 'Given your so-called "trade", you leave your home open to search any day. What do you expect?'

'Leaving your guesses regarding myself out of it, I expect respect for women and children from any man. What I came here to say is this: if in future any man of yours lays a hand on my wife, he'll lose it. *That* I promise you. So let them know it, Captain.' He turned about and was gone before Penn could reply.

That the man's words had held the authority of truth, Penn was forced to recognize. The memory of the encounter remained to fester in his mind. That there had been a successful run of contraband into the area under his control, he knew, though the only proof of it was the half-anker Saul Wadey had found. He had used the finding of the disused stowholes near Ryland's cottage as an excuse as much as a reason for sending a detail to search it. He could admit to himself that it had been a personal satisfaction to do so. Now. . . . Penn's hands clenched on the desk. Whatever it took, he would see Ryland paid the price. If it were in any way possible, when he caught him it would be with evidence that would hang him.

His thoughts turned to the Irishman, Johnston, the immediate cause of the latest mischief. Had they been at sea, he would have the man flogged for exceeding his orders. He could dismiss him for persistent drunkenness. And there was another mystery: where did the man obtain a supply of liquor extra to the daily grog allowance? But the truth of the matter was he could not afford to dismiss the man because there was no guarantee that a replacement would be made, or that he would be a better man. With the hours of darkness already lengthening and a tight roster, he could not afford to lose even a man so little to be depended on as Johnston.

The captain's white fury kept everyone around him on tiptoe for the rest of the evening.

Mrs Timson, unremarkable in every way except as one of Elswick's most comfortably circumstanced inhabitants, had been in expectation of a visit from her nephew and niece for several weeks. They arrived on a Saturday and on Sunday, anyone who chose to linger on the church path after morning service, could judge if the rumour, already current, of the brother and sister's exceptional good looks was true.

It was Elise's opinion that for once report had fallen short of the truth: the golden beauty of the brother and sister was startling. Their likeness to each other suggested that they might be twins but the report was that Miss Irma Rivardeau was twenty-one, her brother Alexander, twenty-three.

Of the two, Elise thought, it was Irma's face that showed the greater maturity but she did not find that unusual given the different rates of development between the sexes. Both were endowed with splendid figures. Irma was a little tall for a woman but still lacked three inches of her brother's height. Their almost faultless features would have made them noticeable in any company, but it was their colouring that made them extraordinary: hair, brows, lashes and skin, all seemed to be washed in varying shades of gold, even the irises of their eyes showed as deep amber, emphasized in each case by a dark outer margin. To all this overplus was added a glowing vitality and a noticeably patrician air. If they knew their worth it was hardly surprising, Elise concluded.

'What a splendid pair they make,' said a voice over Elise's

shoulder. It was said generously with just the smallest sigh of envy.

Elise, waiting for the Woodstows who were in conversation with the vicar, turned to see the vicar's daughter, Mary Staunton, smiling at her. A plain young woman and at twenty-six seemingly settled into spinsterhood, and quite unsoured by it. Already there was liking established between them and Elise smiled back warmly at her.

'Was I staring? How remiss of me. But they do so take the eye. The wonder is that they have survived to their present ages unwed. They shine us all down, don't they?'

'But not to the point of putting you in eclipse Miss Hilliard.'

Elise laughed and shook her head. 'Now that is being too kind. I fear there can be very few young women who are not eclipsed in Miss Rivardeau's presence. I cannot pretend to beauty and put beside her, at my very best I could not look better than a tallow-dip beside the finest wax candle.'

'I cannot agree with you,' Miss Staunton returned staunchly. 'It is very much to their credit though, that looking as they do, they appear so little conscious of superiority. They will, I think be much in demand.'

'If only judged by the difficulty we are all finding in looking anywhere but at them, I am sure you are right.' She glanced round to see if her cousins were ready to move off, and caught sight of Nicholas Mariott. He, no less than anyone else was gazing at Miss Rivardeau. And like every other man there, his expression showed his reaction to her beauty.

One gentleman at least, whatever his reaction to Miss Rivardeau had been, did not allow it to extinguish his interest in Miss Hilliard.

Captain Penn had not had to wait long for a reply to the letter of enquiry he had sent to his sister, Celia. Blessed with a passionate interest in scandal and a good nose for value, she had been able to inform him that Miss Hilliard had lapsed from the path of virtue and been utterly disgraced, which had been the reason for her hasty departure from Bath. What Mrs Jameson found extraordinary was that the man concerned had not married her despite the fact that she had a fortune of £15,000 left entirely in her own hands by her parents who had died in some epidemic when their daughter was still a schoolgirl. There was a rumour – though it was nothing more substantial than that – that she might be possessed of even more through a legacy from her godmother.

To a man worth no more than £2,000 in hard-won prize money, £15,000 could be an acceptable compensation for something less than perfection in a bride.

Riding his undistinguished hack,Penn was some distance away when he saw Elise close the gates of Greenaleigh House behind her and turn towards the village. When he drew level with her and dismounted, she stopped to greet him with a smile and offer her hand.

He fell in beside her, leading his horse and showing every evidence of being pleased with the meeting.

When the commonplaces began to flag, Elise said, 'You must find the bricks and mortar of your new quarters an improvement over canvas with the weather now so unsettled.'

'Indeed.'

'I have sometimes seen your men keeping their lonely watch without shelter and cannot help but feel sorry for them,' she added.

'Most seamen are hardened to foul weather. I am not without sympathy for their plight, but there is no choice in the matter. The Admiralty sets the rule and keeping watch is the purpose of our being here. This Sussex coast is all too well suited to the smugglers' purposes.' He slanted a wry look at her. 'What the men find harder to endure is being cut off from ordinary communication with the people around them and being reviled for doing their duty. I feel it – and I am in a more privileged position. You said when we spoke at our first meeting that you had no firm opinion regarding smuggling. Was that all the truth? Or do you at heart have sympathy with the smugglers, as many do?'

She gave some thought to her answer before saying, 'What is

certain is that I do not know very much about it. I suppose I feel some sympathy for those who see smuggling as a means of getting a livelihood . . . who depend on it.'

'Which could be said by any cutpurse, sneak-thief or house-breaker. Smugglers rob the nation of its revenues. And it is a brutal trade, with a vicious reputation.'

She thought of Josh Ryland, who was reputed to be the smug-glers' leader. Brutal? Vicious? She had seen a very favourable side of him, but what did she really know of him? She said doubtfully, 'As I told you, I know little about it.'

He smiled down at her. 'And do not mean to argue it with me. . . .'

She inclined her head in assent and gestured towards a footpath that led past the Sussex Oak. 'In any case I must leave you here. I am expected at the manor-house.'

'Then when we meet again I shall hope to be more successful in persuading you of the justice of the navy's cause – indeed, the country's cause.' He took her hand, bowed over it, hesitated, then said, 'Captain is a courtesy title given to all officers who command a shore-party. My true rank is that of first lieutenant.' He touched his hat and turned to remount.

Walking the short distance to the manor gates, Elise was thoughtful. Penn had made a plain show of his cards. Did it please her or not? It was much too soon to know, she decided.

When the Irishman, Johnston, was next on night duty, Midshipman Surtees thought it bad luck that he should be the patrolling officer.

Penn had deprived the man of his rum ration following the raid on the Rylands' cottage and though he obtained some liquor from another source, he was surly and resentful. The chance was, Surtees thought, that Johnston would remember who it was had reported his behaviour to Penn. The man was born a bully, his behaviour unpredictable at the best of times.

Trudging the mile of his surveillance in the fitful dark of another windy night in which the waxing moon dodged in and out of the clouds, Surtees spoke in turn to each of the men spaced out on their lonely vigil, excepting only Johnston. It was enough, the young midshipman told himself, to see that the man was awake, on his feet and appeared to be doing what he should.

Johnston was second in the line of men. Surtees had crossed the stubble field fifty yards behind the Irishman, noting that he appeared unaware of his officer's presence. He plodded on to where the last man was stationed, exchanging a few words with him before turning and beginning the walk back. Reaching the stubble field again, he could not locate Johnston. The moon was in hiding, the shadows deep. Surtees moved down the field closer to where Johnston should be and where the land ended. The wind was coming in strongly off the sea, wet with spume blown from the white-caps. It was not until Surtees lowered his gaze to the ground that he saw Johnston, a dark shape just visible against the paleness of the reaped field. Asleep, dammit! Asleep on duty. This time he was for it. First, though, he had to be wakened.

Five years in the navy had taught Surtees what was expected of an officer. It did not make what had to be done any easier. He was no more than averagely tall for his age and his figure was slight. Johnston had both height and bulk. From a distance of two or three yards, he called the man's name. There was no response. He walked nearer, nudged the prone figure with the toe of a boot. He heard a whimpering groan, but there was no movement.

'On your feet, Johnston,' Surtees commanded, with all the authority he could muster. There was another groan, but still no movement. It was then Surtees realized that Johnston was not wearing his jacket, it was simply spread over him. He bent down and lifted the garment away. With it came the man's shirt which appeared also to have been laid across his back. Momentarily, the moon sailed clear of clouds, drifting a pallid light across the field before vanishing again. It had been enough to show Surtees the dark criss-cross of weals across Johnston's back. The Irishman had been flogged.

How long since Surtees had last seen him? To the last sentinel and back was more than a mile; a slow walk in poor light over uneven ground. Time enough for it to happen. Surtees bent again and gripping the man's shoulder, said urgently, 'Get up, Johnston. You need to get back to the watch-house.'

A growl was all he got in return. There was no way he could hoist the heavy seaman to his feet. He laid shirt and coat back where they had been and made a hurried return to the watch-house for help.

Brought back to base, sullen and sour, Johnston, his weals anointed with salve by one of his peers who stood in for the visiting medical officer, and with a tot of rum granted him by Surtees, he gave a bare, grudging outline of what had happened. Unseen and unheard until too late, four men had overpowered and gagged him. Then he had been frog-marched to the nearest gate, his upper garments removed, his arms spread wide and his wrists lashed to the top bar. Two of the men had then administered the flogging. Afterwards, he had been dragged back to where Surtees had found him and there left. His attackers had all worn mufflers around their faces to their eyes and seamen's woollen bonnets drawn low over their brows. No chance to recognize any of them. And not a word spoken among them from beginning to end.

Penn was given a report early the following morning. There could be only one reason for the selection of Johnston for what was clearly intended as punishment. And that led back to Joshua Ryland.

It was no surprise to Penn that probing enquiries throughout the village only resulted in what seemed like half its inhabitants having witnessed Ryland putting to sea in his lugger on the outgoing tide the previous afternoon. Seemingly, he had not yet returned.

Penn had no regret for what had happened to Johnston except

as it affronted his own authority. The man had got what he deserved. He would have fared worse had he received a naval flogging. What chafed him through and through was his inability to prove that Ryland had any direct connection with it.

CHAPTER SEVEN

At the beginning of the third week of November the wind swung south-west, coming in across the land with a high thin whine and enough power to strip the last leaves from what trees there were and bend them like a conquered people cringing before their victors.

The sea darkened, driven landward in long heaving rollers to give seemingly permanent high tides. Before long the rollers became a wild convulsion of breakers that battered down walls, ripped boats from their moorings and flooded the low-lying land.

Gale succeeded gale with only a few hours between when an eerie stillness replaced the clamour that had preceded it. By nightfall on the twenty-third, the storm that hit the southern coast reached hurricane strength. Sea and sky merged in a black, roaring tumult and the air inland was a salt vapour from blown spume.

Penn called in his sentinels. Outside, men could barely stand erect against the force of the wind and visibility was almost nil. Nevertheless, he posted two men to watch seaward in what shelter a porch offered; a dog-watch of two hours to be endured until others took over. Any ship that had not made harbour was in danger of coming ashore as a wreck.

When the first dog-watch was relieved, the men reported that once or twice in the last half-hour they thought they had glimpsed a tossing glimmer of light somewhere in the black boil seaward. But in such conditions, the eyes played tricks; they could not be sure. But men going fresh to the second watch soon were sure. There was a vessel somewhere in that hell of wind and water that was being driven shoreward with little resistance from its own helm.

A ship in danger of foundering bound all seamen in brother-hood and Penn had no difficulty mustering a party to give any possible help. When they reached the nearby low headland it was approaching midnight. Local seamen were there before them.

Penn was weighing the chances of any help reaching the vessel, when a hand was laid on his shoulder and a voice shouted above the roar of wind and surf, 'A schooner, at a guess. She's low enough in the water to be half full of it already. She was lucky to miss Selsey Bill but she'll founder before she strikes land and then God help them all! A galley out to her with a prayer or two is the most hope for her.'

Ryland's voice, Penn recognized. His words matched Penn's thought. But the chance of a galley surviving that hellish combi-nation of the elements, let alone making a rescue, was hard to believe in. Yet an attempt had to be made. With something to be done, Penn could detach himself from personal animosity and he answered Ryland as he would any other man. 'Yes. We'll be launching our galley immediately.'

'You'll not do it out of the harbour, Captain. There's a tangle of boats and wrecks blocking the entrance. But I have a galley right here, bigger and stronger than yours. She's clinker-built and eight oars to your galley's six.' The note of laughter that so irritated Penn was back in his voice. 'With the sea topping the land, we can launch her straight from the field.'

It made sense and it was a time for quick decisions. Penn said, 'Right. Show me.'

'If you've any thought of coming with us, Captain, forget it.' Ryland was speaking seriously again. 'How long since you handled an oar? Not since your midshipman days, I'd guess. It's work for me. I know the seas, the currents, the coast, as you cannot. When we return – if we do' – his teeth gleamed through the murk in a grin – 'we'll need someone here who can see how best to get us ashore. It won't be the easiest part. We'll be making for The Bend. Hit or miss. If we're ditched then, it'll be a comfort to know you're here to pull us from a watery grave. If you can.'

He was already moving and Penn followed. He saw the galley only at the last moment. Several feet longer than the permitted twelve . . . not only clinker-built, but black. A smuggler's boat and illegal on all three points.

Josh turned. 'The tiller's lashed and I've five unmarried men and myself to take oars. I'm taking no married men if I can help it. Have you three unmarried who'll come with us? Two will need to be both strengthy and good oarsmen. The third to bale.'

'I'll find them.'

As Penn turned to go, Josh drew forward a stripling who had been pinned like a shadow to his shoulder. 'Tell your mother a light in every seaward window as bright as can be made, particularly upstairs. And tell her to stay within and tend them. No going down to The Bend.'

'Right. But *I* shall be there,' the youth said, in something close to Josh's hardy tone.

'About that, you'll do as you please. But keep an eye on your mother.' He laid a hand on the boy's shoulder and they looked at each other for a long moment of deep intimacy and though neither said more, all that was needed passed between them. Then Josh nodded and they turned and moved in opposite directions.

Among his own men, Penn found three who were unmarried, or who said they were, and who were ready, even eager, to take what was far beyond any ordinary risk.

Willing helpers struggled to keep upright on the muddy grassy land in a seethe of water past their knees. They had both to propel the black boat to the land's edge and hold it back from the sea, bucking and rearing as though possessed of a devil, while the rowers did their best to scramble into it.

'We'll hope to cut the line the vessel out there is likely being carried,' Josh said to Penn, as he stood ready to step into the galley. Penn nodded. Then, struck by sudden recollection, he said, *'You're* a married man.'

Again, Josh grinned at him. 'But blessed with three sons. My eldest fifteen – near enough a man. And two who think they are.' With that, he heaved himself into the galley and taking his place at an oar, stared seaward across his shoulder. When the next big wave came in, rising and breaking as it met the submerged shoulder of land, he waited for the surge to spend itself, then bellowed 'Now!' Those holding the boat threw all their force into thrusting it as far forward as possible into the savage turmoil of deeper water.

'God go with you!' a voice yelled hoarsely. But there was a long moment in which the galley seemed to hang poised as though waiting to be flung back. Oars stubbornly fighting the sea, the boat was inched away from the land. Fifty yards out, black on black, it's position could not even be guessed.

Nothing now for those on shore to do but trudge to The Bend and wait with their ropes, boathooks and storm lanterns, to gaze at the mist-blurred beacon made by the lighted windows of the only cottage nearby and then to stare with aching, salt-stung eyes into the black void beyond the pale blown spray of the nearest breakers in the frail hope of glimpsing the lights carried by the endangered ship. That, and to feel the leaden weight of time, with nothing but prayer to prop up hope.

The church protected the vicarage with its bulk, south and west, making it on this tempestuous night one of the quieter and least affected houses in the village. An hour short of the time when dawn might be expected to arrive but probably would not, the church bell began to clang. Shredded by the wind, it was still enough to shake the vicar awake and aware of the tumult outside. He rose, dressed and went downstairs to find his daughter there before him, wrapped in cloak and hood and about to go to the church.

As her father came down into the hall, Mary Staunton said,

'The storm is very bad, I can see nothing outside it is so black. Perhaps someone is using the bell as an alarm. A fire, possibly, though in this wind I pray not.'

'Indeed, God forbid! You have a lantern. Good. We'll go together.' Though the vicar was now only in his mid-fifties, when they opened the side door nearest to the church and stepped out into the wildness of the night, it did not occur to him to send his daughter back into the shelter of the house. Death having robbed him of his wife, he had long ago accepted that it was right and proper for Mary to take care of him in her place. He took her arm as much for his own balance as hers. A careful shepherd of his flock, an innate selfishness made him a poor father.

The clamour of wind and bell together conveyed an odd idea of panic and made them thankful to reach the muffling protection of the church. Inside, the small glow of a single candle led them to the bell-tower where they found St Cuthbert's oldest bellringer pulling with desperate energy and a distressing shortness of breath on the thick rope.

'What in the world are you doing, Paterson?' the vicar demanded.

'Laying the storm,' gasped the elder, without breaking his rhythm. 'My boy's out there in such seas as never was and 'tis the only way.'

'That old superstition! You should know better.' The vicar was irritated. 'Stop pulling that rope at once and put your trust in God.'

The bellringer paused, but held on to the rope as he directed a tigerish glare at the other man. 'I've seen it work. And maybe God needs a nudge. Meaning no disrespect.'

Mary looked at him with sympathy. The son he spoke of, late come and the only one, was thirty if a day, but to his father, he was still a boy to be worried about. 'Let him ring, Papa,' she urged quietly. 'It will do no harm and thinking that he is doing something to help his son obviously comforts him.'

'Oh, very well. Carry on, if you must, Paterson. But you're

76

doing yourself no good and prayer would serve you better.'

The vicar turned away and stalked in silence back to the house.

Mary saw with relief there was a light in the kitchen window which meant their two servants were up to give her father the cosseting he would now expect. She suspected there was a homily in the making for her and when they reached the door, she turned away, saying, 'I will go and see what can be found out. Someone may need our help.' She was gone quickly enough to avoid argument.

Penn had made the best provision he could against the black boat's return though he had little faith in it. In The Bend, as everywhere else, the sea was well up over the lip of the land. Here, the coast sloped back slightly north-east so that the western arm of the minute cove jutted out to give it a small degree of protection. How much difference it made tonight was not perceptible to the eye. Penn pushed back those of the watchers who could be of no use and placed his own men to hold them there, leaving a wide corridor of clear ground with ropes, boathooks, grappling irons, anything that might be of use, laid to hand. After that, there was nothing to be done except endure the slow passage of time and strain the eyes seaward more in hope than expectation of seeing sign of a returning boat.

There had been no glimpse of light anywhere for a long, long time when a sour yellow streak cut a line through the darkness, the first herald of a late dawn. There were women among the watchers now, but hope – ridiculous though it had been from the beginning – was ebbing fast. Ryland and those who went with him, must have known that what they were attempting was sheer suicidal lunacy, Penn thought. Now there were nine more men to add to the loss of whatever number the foundering ship had carried. And but for Ryland's intervention, he, Penn, would have been among them. He wondered what it was that drew men so inexorably to lost causes, impossible odds? And they had waited to the last gasp of hope and beyond. It was time to gather

77

his men and gear together and go.

Others, reaching the same dismal conclusion, began to drift away. The wonder was that so many had stood through the long hours, breathing only a salt vapour, soaked to the skin and numbed almost to insensibility by cold.

While his men were sorting their irons from those owned by the locals, Penn grappled with problems that lay ahead. He had lost three of his best, most dependable men. Belatedly it came to his tired mind that, without Ryland, smuggling in Elswick could dwindle to an end. He would reap no glory from that. Depression flowed in. He was as wet and chilled as any other man despite his oilskins. There was small comfort to be found at the watch-house – none at all to be found in remaining here in this bleak, despondent dawn. . . .

'Something . . . I saw something, I swear!' a voice shrilled through the watchers' lethargy.

A young voice, with which went the probability of keen eyes. Was it possible? Penn raised his telescope and was surprised to find it had stopped raining and the darkness was no longer absolute. He swept the glass across what was visible seaward. Nothing. And again nothing. And then suddenly, miraculously, there *was* something. A boat, heavy laden, wallowing shoreward on the driving, cross-running flood, oars fighting more to hold a course than used for propulsion. There was cheering now, an eagerness to push forward. Penn roared at the crowd to stand back.

Nothing could be done before the boat came close enough to be reached with hook, hand or grapple and Penn knew, as Ryland had, that this would be far from easy to do. Rowers and survivors must be in the last stage of exhaustion, while for those on the inundated land, one step too many could lead to a man plunging down with nothing beneath his feet and swept beyond rescue in seconds.

Penn watched the galley with a professional eye, trying to

assess its chance of actually entering the meagre curve of The Bend. Only luck and superb seamanship could have brought it through such seas to their present position. By a breath-stoppingly narrow margin, the same combination brought it in. Penn found himself releasing held breath in a long exhalation.

His part now was to be ready to make split-second decisions to meet whatever last nightmare of difficulty the sea had in waiting.

Janus-faced, what it did, was send in a roller that broke short and left the boat snagged on the lip of the land to hang there perilously, threatening to tip all in it backwards into the water. But even as the bow began its lift, with some guide now to the edge of the land, Penn had men reaching to grapple her with hands, hooks and irons and to haul her forward, bring her clear.

The boats' human cargo fell rather than climbed out, helped and supported by rough, willing hands pushing and pulling each man to safety where he immediately collapsed just beyond reach of the salt flood. Even Joshua Ryland sat limp and drooping, at the end of his strength, his hands, hardened and calloused as they normally were by rugged use, hanging raw and bloody between his knees.

It was Ben Saulter, the innkeeper, plying rescued and rescuers alike with brandy from the half-anker he had brought down to The Bend, who first restored some semblance of life among them. Others followed, ministering to their needs with food and blankets, Nick Mariott and his housekeeper among them.

Gradually, as some of the rescued crew recovered strength enough to speak, it emerged that the ship had been the Dutch schooner, *Yonge Berta*. She had been caught by the storm when returning from making a delivery of apples and cheeses to Cork where she had taken on a catch-cargo of linen intended for delivery to London before returning to the home port of Amsterdam. Captain and men expressed their gratitude for rescue in tones too heartfelt to be misunderstood whether they spoke in Dutch or broken English. Thanks to their smuggling activities, some of the Elswick seamen present had a smattering of Dutch. These were

79

able to pass on the information that the Dutchmen had lost five of their number, four overboard and one in the hazardous transfer from ship to boat. The *Yonge Berta* had sunk almost under the feet of her captain who, in the best tradition, had been the last man to leave her.

Penn went to speak to the three navy men who had accompanied Ryland. Two attempted to struggle to their feet but he waved them down. 'Well done, all of you,' he said. 'Glad to see you survived, though I hardly expected it. I'll see you reap some benefit from this night's work.'

So much from Penn was not the least of the night's miracles. It prompted Thompson, once a topgallant man and the oldest of the group, to a more expansive reply than he might otherwise have ventured upon.

Nodding to where Josh sat with the Dutch captain, apparently in fairly fluent converse, the seaman said, 'That man's a devil possessed when he wills to do a thing, sir. It's not so much he drives men as he carries them with him.' He was tempted to add, 'unlike some I know', but did not. Penn was a good officer, one to be depended on, but he was not one to draw men's liking, nor one with whom they could be easy. The man went on, 'When the Dutchies held back from making the crossing into the boat – and God knows I didn't blame them – he roared at them in their own tongue and ours with words as brought them over like scolded children. And that even after they'd lost a man.'

Penn nodded and turned away. Could he have done as well? He thrust the question from him. Though no coward, he was aware of being glad that, in the end, he had not had to try. A second measure of brandy was thrust into his hand by the innkeeper and he drank it thankfully, but this time woke to awareness of its velvet smoothness. The best there was, and contraband for a certainty. In the grey but strengthening light, his gaze caught up with Saulter. With more humour in his make-up he might have smiled at the realization. As it was, grateful though he was for the brandy's bracing warmth, he marked it down as one more instance of the cool effrontery of these Sussex men.

The crowd was beginning to disperse, sharing rescued Dutchmen among themselves as they went. Three of them were too weak to stand and Penn ordered them to be carried to the watch-house to be cared for and his own three men who had gone with Ryland to accompany them, to eat and to rest. The Dutch captain and his first mate had accepted an offer of hospitality from Ryland. Another irritation. Tiredly, he straightened his shoulders, impatient of any sign of weakness in himself. Then memory woke and he looked to where he expected to see the black galley. It was not there. Nor was it anywhere else within view. Occupied with other things, he had been entirely unconscious of its removal. Angry that he had not thought of it sooner, he crossed to where Josh was pushing himself up on to his feet. Something was due to the man from himself and must be paid.

Approaching, he said stiffly, 'You and those who went with you are to be congratulated on a considerable feat of seamanship. But you in particular, so I'm told.'

The difficulty the captain must have had to bring himself to say as much put a smile on Josh's face, though it was a crooked one. 'Those who went with me were all first-rate seamen, yours and mine, Captain. Maybe we were lucky, or maybe the seaman's saints lent us aid. There's more than a handful of those, by all accounts, and I reckon we needed every one.'

In Penn's view, Ryland's man-to-man easiness when speaking to him implied an inability to perceive a difference in status and, as always, irritated him. His voice hardened and he said, 'All the same, Ryland, tonight makes no difference to where we both stand. I shall be looking for that black galley of yours.'

'I never expected different.'

Josh grinned widely at him adding to Penn's resentment. It drove him on to say, 'The navy could make good use of your kind of seamanship. If you don't finish at the end of a rope first, I'll see it has benefit of it for at least five years. So keep it in mind.'

Josh's weary face creased with laughter. 'Tell me again when you've caught me, Captain.'

CHAPTER EIGHT

The storm woke Elise in the early hours. She lay for a while listening to the ferocity of the night outside, the unidentifiable crashes and bangs of destruction near and far. After a while, knowing she would not return to sleep, she rose, lit her candle, dressed, and went downstairs. Standing in the hall, for the moment undecided what to do, she was drawn towards the kitchen by sound of activity there. Entering, she found the cook in nightcap and immense wrapper sitting at the table, and Millie, one of the housemaids, in nightgown and shawl and a thick plait of gingery hair over one shoulder, pouring tea into thick cups from a brown-glazed teapot.

Popular with the Greenaleigh staff, Elise was welcomed in and offered tea and bread and butter which she gladly accepted.

Safe in a well-built house and now with an audience, the two servants could repeat all that they had already said of the raging elements. Not being 'local' or having sea-faring menfolk, they could speak, too, of their fear for ships caught at sea without any depth of anxiety.

Before long, Elise grew restless and when at last, she saw from a window the first acid streak of light cutting the black canopy of cloud, she left the kitchen and, wrapping herself in a thick cloak belonging to Cousin Matthew, tied a scarf about her head and despite the two servants' fearsome predictions of the dangers awaiting her, went out to discover what ills the storm had brought to the village.

The storm was no longer at its peak, but it was still rough and wild and though the rain had stopped, the air was heavily damp and salt. Bobbing lantern-lights drew her by way of the footpath to The Bend and there she found many all too willing to give her animated accounts of the rescue. The throng was beginning to disperse and looking round in the first dimly sallow light she saw Nicholas Mariott on the outer edge standing as though waiting for something or someone. Wanting a plainer tale of the night's happenings than she had yet heard, she was moving towards him when she saw Joshua Ryland with two men and a boy on a converging path towards him and slowing, she hesitated. As the three approached, Josh in the lead, Nicholas Mariott held out his hand.

With dismay, Elise saw the tall seaman walk past him as though he were invisible. The two men accompanying him glanced curiously at the waiting man and hurriedly looked away. The boy, too, after one flying, startled glance, turned his gaze forward and walked after the rest.

The strength of her indignation on Nicholas Mariott's behalf surprised Elise. Whatever lay between the two men, it had been a cruel rejection. She felt she had learned enough about Nicholas Mariott to guess his pride to be both fragile and fiery. Yet he had laid it in the palm of the hand he had offered Joshua Ryland; a measure perhaps of the value he set upon him. Reflected in his face, she saw his first painful reaction to that contemptuous repudiation; saw it fade swiftly away to be replaced by a look so formidable that she took an involuntary step forward as though to ward off some intolerable counterblast. Her dismay deepened. It appeared to her that whatever bitterness of feeling had motivated Joshua Ryland's action had woken something in the other man darker than itself.

It raised a memory of the glitter of emotion that had flashed through Joshua Ryland's eyes when Henry had asked him when he would be friends with his godfather again; she had tried to analyse it but without success. Anger, yes, but something else equally strong. Whatever had driven them apart, both had been deeply scarred by it.

At this moment what seemed to her most important was to turn Nicholas Mariott's mind away from what had happened before the thought and feeling that had put such a look on his face could harden into wicked purpose. To offer sympathy would be an unbearable intrusion: distraction was all she could provide. She closed the small remaining distance separating them. . . .

Josh and Barney Tench met in the Sussex Oak in the early evening of that same day. Barney looked the seaman he was, brown and seamed and calloused. Three years younger than Josh, his brown hair was greying and thinning, but his plain, squarish face held something of the same cheerful acceptance of life as it came. Carrying their tankards of ale to a bench furthest from the scatter of other customers, they sat down and regarded each other with satisfaction.

'Thought we'd lost you. Folks was about to give up and go home when John Tallack's lad cried out he'd seen something,' Barney said.

'We came in on the tide. . . . All we had to do was stay afloat.' Josh grinned at him.

All! Barney, with good knowledge of what 'all' had entailed and what the chances of staying afloat had been, simply shook his head.

Josh rubbed a painful shoulder. 'Never had so many aches in my life.' He looked down at his hands, turning them over to grimace at the sore and swollen palms that Prue had anointed with a virulent green ointment of her own making. 'Never left so much skin on the oar-looms either.' More seriously, he said, 'You got the galley away safe, thank God. I was too spent to think of it soon enough last night. Good work on your part, Barney, because it wasn't long before Penn looked round for it. Did you have any trouble?'

'No, none. We got it into the cradle and had it away while

everyone was still busy with you and the Dutchies and it was still too dark to see much. But don't put the idea of it down to me. It was Mr Mariott. Soon as he came, he took me on one side to say get the galley away before the captain remembers it. And so we did.'

There followed long moments of utter silence before Josh said with chilling ferocity, '*Damn him! Damn him! Damn him!*'

Barney sat staring at the other man in baffled silence until pushed by sheer discomfort into asking, 'What's wrong, Josh?'

Josh came back slowly to the here and now.

'Wrong?' he said harshly. 'Nothing in this world.' He pushed his tankard of ale aside and called to the landlord, 'Ben! We need something stronger here. Bring us some brandy.' He looked back at Barney with glittering eyes, and a smile that held neither pleasure nor humour. 'We'll drink to a day of reckoning, my friend.'

Counting the cost of the storm, Elswick found it heavy. Boats in the harbour and elsewhere had been badly damaged or had vanished altogether. There was damage done to houses and barns, walls had been brought down or cracked, roofs and sheds blown away, some of the latter with the hens and rabbits they had contained. It would be a lean winter for many this year.

Danesfield, too, had suffered, not least from land flooded by salt water, and Nick had plenty to keep him occupied during the next few days. When priorities had been decided and repairs begun, he turned his attention to a matter he had put in hand before the storm and which now took him to Greenaleigh House. Matthew was in his study and Nick joined him there, thankful for Amelia's absence.

The courtesies at an end, he said bluntly, 'It's time Henry had a pony of his own, Matthew. John Hammond has taught him to ride, as you know, but he needs more practice and the convenience of having a mount available when he wants it.'

'Amelia—' Matthew began.

'Yes, I know, Amelia is very conscious of the way in which

86

Henry's father met his death,' Nick headed off what Matthew was about to say. 'It is for that reason I have not pressed the matter earlier. But Henry is old enough to have some sense now and he doesn't have the same neck-or-nothing temperament as his father.'

Seeing trouble ahead, Matthew frowned. 'It's not just a matter of how Charles died. Amelia has this feeling that it is – I don't know – in a way *disrespectful* to his father's memory. She was pretty much put about when you first suggested the boy had a pony, and more so when you had him taught to ride at Danesfield. A woman's crotchet, no doubt, but she feels strongly about it.'

'I respect Amelia's feelings in the matter,' Nick said, which was untrue, 'but being able to ride and to ride well, is a normal part of the upbringing of a boy like Henry. He cannot be allowed to feel out of place among his peers. If you knew anything of Charles, you cannot believe that he would not want his son to ride and to enjoy the pleasure that a boy naturally finds in it.'

Nick regarded Matthew with mild cynicism. 'You need put yourself to no trouble over it. Hammond sought out a neat little Appaloosa for me, well-paced and sweet-tempered, and just right for Henry. Hammond's nephew, Edward, has been working in the Lennox stables but is looking for somewhere to be in sole charge and would welcome a return to Elswick. He's a reliable young man, well trained, and could look for something better than the care of one pony and a hack.'

'A hack?'

'Eddie will need a mount if he is to accompany Henry. I will provide them both and I imagine the trust is able to afford young Hammond's wage.'

Matthew shot him a resentful glance. 'You have got it all laid out, haven't you Nick? Well, I suppose it's got to be, but Amelia isn't going to like it.'

Nick had no further words to say on Amelia's feelings. 'If you're agreeable then, I'll ask John to get in touch with his nephew to tell him to make his arrangements and come to me as soon as he can.

I'll bring him along and you can see what you think of him. Are the rooms over the stables that Charles's man had still available? Christmas is not far off. A good time for Henry to be presented with the pony. If you decide Eddie Hammond suits you, he can spend the day before Christmas preparing the stable for the animals before collecting them from Danesfield.'

He watched Matthew accept his ordering of the affair with ravelled amusement, deploring the man's weakness and his own exploitation of it. But it had been the only way to get the matter moving. Matthew would weigh the lack of trouble to himself against his wife's objections and present the matter to her as having been taken out of his hands in a most overbearing way. Which, of course, it had. He had, too, been careful to refer to the Appaloosa as a 'pony', though in fact it crept by a mere inch into the horse category.

Matthew, not unaware of having been manipulated, attempted a small requital, saying, 'Amelia was very much put about by your housing that dog she did not wish to have about the place.'

'Henry bought the dog with his pocket money. At a very generous discount, I may say. If he chose to offer it to me, he was entitled to do so. It's a valuable animal.' Nick kept his tone light.

'Well. . . .' Matthew let the point slide and rose as Nick did. 'You're off then.' His relief was patent and he made no attempt to detain his visitor.

With Christmas less than three weeks away, those who *could* were determined to enjoy its pleasures. Parties of every kind were got up, increasing in number as the day drew near. As Mary Staunton had predicted, the Rivardeau brother and sister were in great demand especially when it was discovered that they sang very pleasantly in duet and though never putting themselves forward, could be persuaded to perform without false or fussy demurs.

On several Sunday mornings, as the congregation left the church and dawdled on the path, Captain Penn had made a point of briefly engaging the Woodstows in conversation when opportunity offered. He made himself agreeable to all, even Henry, whose patent awe and hero-worship of himself amused him. Without display, he allowed his interest in Elise to show.

Christmas Eve fell on a Sunday this year and two Sundays before this, when Matthew, thinking of his dinner, began to move towards the gate, the captain moved too, continuing a discussion he had begun with Amelia. When he gave signs of parting from them, Amelia, flattered by the attention he had paid her and the respect he had shown her opinions, invited him to dine with them. Dinner, she explained, was eaten early on Sundays so that the servants might complete their duties in time to attend evening service.

The captain accepted the invitation with pleasure and proved himself a guest worth having. He did not linger long after the meal, but before there was any chance that his presence might weary them, took his leave pleading the claims of duty.

Four days after, Penn received a letter from Captain McCulloch's office relaying information received from one of the spies he maintained in Boulogne. He read it through twice, hardly able to believe his luck. Two more days passed and he watched *Sea Dancer* put out to sea and a warm tide of satisfaction flowed through him. Eight days to Christmas and *then* the reckoning!

Dressing for the party Mrs Timson was giving for Irma and Alexander Rivardeau, Elise recollected her first opinion of Elswick's ability to provide entertainment. What there was might not have the diversity to be found in Bath, but there was no lack of it, nor of readiness to enjoy it. Even Amelia showed surprising willingness to go wherever invited. In the beginning, Elise had thought that Amelia saw herself in the role of a necessary watchdog. But before long she realized that Amelia, having few friends and being given little companionship by her husband, had a great liking for being in company. Which did not hinder her from finding a self-sacrificing motive for her indulgence.

The Timson invitations had promised dancing and there was no doubt who was to be the belle of the ball. Miss Rivardeau in a gown of cream silk with the new wide, epaulette sleeves, a long amber-coloured sash, her pale hair dressed high and twined with flowers to match her sash drew the men's eyes as surely as the moon draws the tides. Her brother was severely garmented in black and white, providing a splendid foil for his sister and incidentally underlining his own blond good looks.

As soon as her cousins were drawn away to the tables set for those who preferred whist to dancing, Elise sought out Mary Staunton.

'Your smile bodes ill for me,' Mary said, with mock apprehension. 'What have I done wrong?'

'Not a thing. I was thinking how entirely satisfactory it is when friends take one's advice.'

Mary laughed a little shyly. She was in better looks than Elise had yet seen her. Her pretty hair was more softly dressed than usual with a small topknot from which a few gentle curls had been allowed enough freedom to frame her face becomingly.

'Yes. I have done as you bade me. Dressed my hair in the most frivolous manner and not worn a cap, which I confess makes me feel quite abandoned.'

'I cannot think *why* since you are neither a dowager nor old enough to be anyone's chaperon. And you look quite charmingly.'

Changes had been made to Mary's pale-grey evening gown, too, Elise noticed. The insertion of a band of pink velvet had given the fashionable longer length to the bodice and was matched by a wider decorative band at the hem. Pink velvet and curls, too – for Mary Staunton, frivolous indeed! Somehow, vowed Elise, she would see if she could not find a few more ways in which to counteract the unthinking limitations the vicar set on his daughter's life. It was unfair of him to restrict her to being nothing other than a 'handmaiden to grace' – that grace being embodied in himself as a minister. Mary deserved better of him.

'When have we ever been sure on every point, Barney? It is *timing* that will count most. That, and you staying out of sight when you get to Elswick. Remember, it's vital you aren't seen. Lie low in my house and don't go near your own. Don't even send a message to your wife. Andy'll take what messages are necessary. He'll follow instructions to the letter and give you a faithful account of what's been managed. When all's done, get back here as fast as you can.'

He saw Barney on to the first packet-boat out of Boulogne heading for Folkestone and stood for some time watching it plough out into the grey, heaving water. But he was not thinking of Barney. He was thinking of Penn.

Christmas Eve was crisp and starry. Matthew, Amelia, Henry and Elise attended midnight mass, as did most of the inhabitants of Elswick. By chance, Elise saw Prue Ryland and her two younger sons entering the church just ahead of them. Because neither Josh nor Andy came to join them she took particular note of other absentees. Mostly they were men whose faces were familiar but whose names she did not know. There was another absentee however, whose face and name she knew well – Captain Penn.

Were those absences linked? It was not a happy thought for the season of peace and goodwill and she shivered.

Amelia had her household in church again on Christmas morning. The absentees were very much the same as those at the midnight service. Elise wondered if Nicholas Mariott had noticed and if so, what his thoughts were.

Henry had received prayer and hymn books in matching leather covers from Amelia and a large box of assorted games from Matthew. Elise had given him three books: *The Last of the Mohicans* by James Fenimore Cooper and Sir Walter Scott's *Rob Roy* and *The Fortunes of Nigel*. He did not know that he was soon to receive a present to eclipse all others.

Unknown to him, the Appaloosa had been brought to the Greenaleigh stables in the dusk of the previous day. Soon after their return from church it was led to the door of the house by Edward Hammond. Elise and the three Woodstows came out on to the steps to see the surprise that Matthew had told Henry awaited him.

First sight of the handsome white, black-spotted animal that the young groom was holding transfixed Henry. When at last he was able to move, he drew a deep breath and gave voice to a triumphant paean.

'A *Dalmatian* horse! My word! Oh, my *word!*' His pleasure far outreached his vocabulary. He ran full tilt down to the gravel, but there, ever a polite child, he stopped and turned to his cousins. 'Thank you, Uncle, Aunt. Oh, thank you! He is the most beautiful horse I ever saw.'

It cost Matthew something to direct that fervent *Te Deum* to where it was deserved, but he did it. 'Your thanks are due to your godfather, Henry. The pony is his gift to you. But it is not a *Dalmatian* pony, it is an Appaloosa. A favourite with the American Indians, I am told.'

Henry was young but intelligently sensitive to what went on around him even if he did not fully understand. Just for a moment, Elise glimpsed the widening of his eyes, the parting of his lips as though he was about to burst out with something like, *Oh, I might have known. . .!* but either innate courtesy or a budding gift for diplomacy made him bridle his enthusiasm and substitute, 'Oh, I see. Yes, I'll be sure to thank him.'

He turned back to make his gift's acquaintance, touching with worshipping reverence the spotted coat, circling the animal to take in all the glory of his tail and mane which, if not conspicuously splendid were very neatly combed and trimmed and the saddle was decidedly handsome. Finally, he halted to look up at the spruce young groom holding the animal.

'Hallo,' he said, a little shyly. 'Have you come to look after him?'

'Yes, Master Henry. Name's Hammond . . . Edward Hammond.'

'Oh, are you—?'

Hammond was nodding in answer to the question before it was complete. 'Yes. My uncle works for Mr Mariott.'

'What's *his* name?' Henry nodded his head at the Appaloosa.

'That's for you to say, young sir.'

'*Oh!*' Henry's cup of pleasure was running over. Breathlessly, he asked, 'Can I try him out now?'

The groom glanced significantly towards the house and Henry at once darted round to the steps and turn a pleading face to his cousin. 'May I go for a ride on him now, Uncle. He's saddled.'

Taking what profit offered from the occasion, Matthew gave consent before Amelia could object.

His wife had watched the scene with her usual look of dissatisfaction, but rules of conduct did not allow her to dispute her husband's permission before a servant and she had to content herself with a frowning, 'The groom must go with him and they must return before too long.'

Hammond touched fingers to his forelock and moved to give Henry a boost into the saddle. Quietly, with a small grin for the boy, he said, 'My own mount's ready saddled in the stableyard. Thought maybe you'd want to ride out.'

'Thanks.' More widely, Henry grinned back. Henry might have few friends, but their number was growing and he had no difficulty recognizing a possible addition.

Elise watched the groom lead the Appaloosa towards the stable and remained on the steps even when her cousins went inside. There could not be many of its kind in the country, she thought; where and how had Nicholas Mariott managed to find it?

Henry and Hammond reappeared a minute or two later. The young man was now leading his own mount as well as the pony. Henry turned with a huge smile to wave to her and she continued to watch as they walked sedately down the drive. There was something about the groom that suggested to her that his relationship with Henry would be a good one. A pound to a penny the pony would be off the leading-rein the moment the groom was content with Henry's riding ability.

Thinking over the care that had gone into the choice of gift for Henry and the difficulties he must have met finding just the right animal, Elise was forced to concede that Nicholas Mariott had some very good qualities.

As Christmas Day moved to its close, Elise realized she had been half expecting Captain Penn to make time to call at Greenaleigh House if only for a brief visit, but he had not come. Nor did he come the following day. Discovering her feelings hovering between a mild disappointment and pique, she laughed at herself. Who did come were the two Rivardeaus to present Elise with a copy of *The Talisman*. It had been published anonymously the previous year but was strongly rumoured to have been written by Sir Walter Scott. They remained for half an hour, charming them all, but with Alex directing much of his attention to Elise.

'A conquest, Elise?' Matthew quizzed her, when they had gone. 'Or should I say *another* conquest? The gallant captain would be wise to look to his laurels, I think.'

Elise laughed. 'What I think is that you would be unwise to think about either gentleman in such terms, Cousin.'

On New Year's Eve, Nick looked at the guests around his table with satisfaction and congratulated himself on having so sensibly solved the problem of entertaining Amelia and pleasing himself at the same time. Last year, because it was too soon after his father's death to give a party, there had been only Amelia, Matthew and Henry.It had been a dull and irksome evening but a necessary blandishment in gaining his objective which was to include Henry and have him stay at Danesfield for the next week. It was a constant puzzle to him how Amelia had managed to catch Matthew in her net.

He had asked Mrs Timson to act as hostess for him and, of course, had invited her nephew and niece. He wanted to see Irma

Rivardeau's reaction to his home, for whatever failure of affection and understanding there had been between himself and his father, he loved Danesfield deeply. Other guests were the Ansteys and Mary Staunton, who, only two years younger than himself, was an old friend. Her father he tolerated for her sake. Miss Hilliard was naturally included with the Woodstows, and for her sake, he had invited Captain Penn. She appeared to like the man and his attentiveness to her was becoming generally noticed. His own relationship with the captain had never recovered from the short, bitter exchange over Josh Ryland that had followed his intervention on young Saul Wadey's behalf.

Miss Hilliard should be grateful to him, he thought sardonically looking down the table to where she was seated with Penn on one side and Henry on the other. She was looking remarkably handsome tonight, he thought. At the moment she was talking to Henry who, relaxed and smiling, was responding happily. Because it was Henry's first experience of an adult dinner party among people who were not all family he had arranged for him to sit between the two youngest women present and so the boy was privileged to have Miss Rivardeau on his other side. Miss Hilliard was now listening to Henry and appeared perfectly happy to give him her full attention.

He had not been able to distinguish her voice through the general murmur of conversation, but he knew it to be a pretty voice that danced gently on the ear. A quiet voice, too, but then she was a quiet young woman, unusually so for someone who must be considered something of a rebel. A quiet rebel was surely almost a contradiction in terms. He transferred his attention to Miss Rivardeau whose beauty shone in this company as in any she graced. As though she sensed his gaze resting on her, Miss Rivardeau looked towards him just then and gave him a brilliant smile before turning back to Matthew, her other partner. Nick did not feel able to flatter himself that the smile had held any special significance. She was charming to everyone, which was how it should be, of course, but was no help in allowing him to decide

99

whether he had yet caught any part of her interest.

He shook off his introspection and turned dutifully to Amelia.

'I have to go to bed when we leave the table,' Henry said to Elise as the meal drew to a close. 'Will you come and say good-night to me like you do at home?'

'Oh dear. I don't think I can, Henry. You see I'm a stranger in this house and don't know my way around it.'

'You could ask Uncle Nick. I'm sure he'd show you.'

'Yes, I'm sure he would. But I don't think I could do that. It's difficult to explain because it's one of those odd grown-up things. I don't know your uncle very well, you see, and it might appear encroaching.' And that, above all things, was something to be avoided.

A request for direction seemed to Henry a very simple matter. He was too polite to press Elise for what he wanted, but he had his own way of achieving his ends. When the time came, he made the round of the guests to say goodnight, ending with his godfather. Nick walked with him to the door of the room and there reminded him to make a wish for the New Year.

'Well, I've got a wish now,' Henry said. 'It's not a very big one but I'd like to have it tonight. I mean it's only *for* tonight.' He looked up hopefully at Nick.

'I suspect I know what it is and it's waiting for you in your room.'

Too intent on pursuing his present objective, Henry did not pause to examine that statement but said, 'Oh, no, she can't be. She's over there talking to Lady Anstey and Captain Penn.'

'*She!*' Nick was startled. He glanced across the room and saw that the 'she' indicated was Miss Hilliard.

'Cousin Elise always comes to say good-night to me when I'm in bed at home, but she doesn't know the way to my room here and she said you'd think she was being enco– *encroaching* if she asked,' Henry explained.

'Did she.' Nick's tone told Henry nothing he understood. 'Well,

100

New Year wishes are meant to come true, so we'll see what can be done about it. Now trot away upstairs yourself, youngling.'

When Lady Anstey left them, Penn said to Elise, 'I shall have to take my leave of you all very soon. Duty calls, alas.'

'The navy makes heavy demands on its people, doesn't it? Even at Christmas. Or were you able to find time to enjoy some part of it?'

An expression she could not interpret crossed Penn's face; a dark look that had something of anger in it. It was gone so quickly she thought she must have misread it, because he was smiling as he said, 'There was no leave for any of us at Christmas. And the business that kept us occupied then is the same as that which will occupy us tonight.'

'Are you speaking of our smugglers.'

'*Any* smugglers that come to this area, but particularly local ones, of course. It is the reason we are here. But *our* smugglers, Miss Hilliard? That sounds more partisan than when I last spoke with you on the subject.'

'No more, no less, I think. Our smugglers simply because they are local.'

'I'm relieved. But preferable to your remaining neutral, I should like to think you were beginning to see there is *right* on our side. The navy's side. *Mine.*' Penn looked at her intently, his voice low and earnest.

Elise glanced away from him. 'As I think I said before, smuggling and its prevention are not matters about which I feel competent to make judgements.'

'Putting that aside then, may I hope you have some kind feelings towards me?'

She gave him a brief, searching look, then said lightly, 'I can say only that I have no *unkind* feelings towards you, Captain.'

'Then I shall hope to improve on that.' He lightened his tone to match hers, took her hand in his and bowed over it. 'It is time for me to go, so I will say goodbye to you now, as I also must do to the rest of the company. Think of me with as much positive kindness as you can meanwhile.'

He had taken a very definite step towards her and she needed to think about it. She was given no time to do so immediately because hardly had the captain left her than Mr Mariott was beside her with a glint in his dark eyes, as though he had seen and sensed something of the intimacy of those last moments with Penn.

'If you are at liberty and would be so good as to go into the hall, Miss Hilliard,' he said very smoothly, 'you will find my housekeeper waiting to conduct you to young Henry's bedroom. I believe you are in the habit of saying good-night to him after he has said his prayers.' He let a moment pass before adding with a slight edge to his words, 'I do assure you, I would never suspect you of encroaching in any way upon me or mine.'

Elise felt the colour rush into her cheeks. 'Oh, the little wretch! How could he!'

'Henry is a faithful intelligencer.' He gave her a smile that told her how well he understood what she felt before walking to the door and opening it for her. She passed him with a very dignified bow.

Danesfield was a long low house and the wide, handsome stairway led to a handsome upper hall from which the door to Henry's bedroom opened. There the pleasant, middle-aged housekeeper left her after being assured she could find her way back to the drawing-room unaided.

Henry was sitting up in a huge four-poster bed, grinning with pleasure. Beside him, a grin almost as wide on his white face framed by elegant, black-spotted ears, sat Dotty, his master's arm around his shoulders.

'Well,' said Elise, walking towards the bed. 'A pair of rascals together! Each accomplished in the art of getting his own way!'

'Yes,' agreed Henry, with rapturous honesty. 'But then Uncle Nick's an absolute *trump*, isn't he?'

102

Though Elise smiled in apparent agreement with Henry, she kept her thoughts concerning Nick Mariott to herself.

CHAPTER TEN

Josh had a sailor's mistrust of Lady Luck being open-handed. The Channel crossing had been too smooth, too easy, a demonstration of the sea's sly capacity always to surprise. Everything so far had been in their favour, a crow-black night, a light sea and a following wind. For the first night of the New Year it was more than anyone could reasonably have hoped for.

They were close to landfall now and the lugger, half-reefed, was running in towards the Sussex coast on a making tide with the wind still favourable. The tide, at least, had been planned for.

In the darkness, the land ahead was more guessed at than seen. It was midnight and somewhere to larboard, Elswick slept, no single light visible seaward.

'Send the signal, Archie,' Josh said to the dark outline of a man standing nearby, and a frail glimmer of light was sent into the night, white, red, white. He wondered if this was where the luck ran out . . . if Penn was waiting in ambush for them. But the answering signal came almost at once, colours reversed, mere pinpricks in the darkness, red, white, red.

Sharp-keeled, lug-sailed but with a top-sail, *Sea Dancer* was fast and manoeuvrable but she was broad and deep of hull and needed a certain depth of water beneath her. The waters here were treacherously shallow in places with shifting sandbars, and knowing the tide would turn soon after 1.30, Josh had her hoved-to at a safe distance from the shore. Before the last dark sail was fully reefed and the ship's boat lowered, the black galley shot out of the night to lay alongside ready to ferry the first part of the cargo ashore.

It was now that timing became critical, with little more than an hour allowed them to get the goods ashore, the cart and ponies loaded and away to their inland destination. If all had gone as it should, the last man in Penn's extended line of sentinels stretching towards Pagham had been put out of action with no chance to fire one of the two useful pistols that lately the navy had made available for issue to men going on watch duty. The pistols were of a new kind, much shorter in the barrel than the old naval issue and easier to handle.

With long practice, the off-loading was done smoothly, quickly and with the minimum of noise. Josh went ashore with the last load. Like the others, he wore a woollen hat pulled low on his brow and a muffler swathing his face to leave only his eyes exposed. If the worst came to the worst and some of the contraband had to be abandoned, the men stood a better chance of melting into the night without being recognized.

Barney appeared at Josh's elbow as soon as he stepped on to land to tell him that half the goods landed had gone on their way, the wheels and hooves of the transport that had been waiting for them well-greased and wrapped against sound.

'They got the navy man neat and tidy,' he added. 'He's up yonder, safely gagged and anchored.'

'No trouble?'

'No. A young one. Midshipman. Sixteen, maybe. Not much weight to him. Here are his pistols.'

Taking them, Josh stuffed them absently into his belt. 'Good. Let's get the rest of the cargo on the road and the goods for Elswick out of the bothy and into the well.'

There was little left to do now. Ten minutes more and the last of the goods, those for distribution in Elswick, would be transferred to the old dry well hidden in bushes beyond all chance of easy finding.

Josh stood in the inner room of the windowless bothy and in the dim light of the dark-lantern standing on a ledge projecting from one of the crumbling walls, looked round with distaste. It had been built, he knew, a century or more ago to house itinerant workers at harvest-time. Apart from walls and a roof, the ledge was the only suggestion that the place had ever contained any contribution to convenience, let alone comfort. Since then it had known a variety of uses. The earth floor had a thin layer of rotting straw and at some time in the intervening years someone had erected a crude door between the two rooms. Nothing indicated that the place had served any recent purpose and the place stank of damp and decay. The wonder was that it was still standing.

Barney Tench and Archie Nye were attending to the disposal of the last few pieces before he and they joined the rest of the men who had already returned to the lugger. Before first light tomorrow, the tenant farmer who worked the land would drive his few head of over-wintering cattle into the bothy and around it to obliterate any trace of the night's activities. He had been paid enough to ensure thoroughness.

Josh found no humour in the recollection that this was Danesfield land . . . Nick's land. He was using it without his knowledge or permission: he would ask no favours from *Mr Mariott*. The last one – unsought – the safe disposal of the black boat after the big storm, had cut deep into his pride. Taking without asking was a different matter and running in here, under Penn's nose, had seemed to have a kind of illogical sense. So far the luck had held.

He pulled the muffler down and wiped a hand tiredly over his face before taking his heavy timepiece out of its pocket and carrying it across to the dark-lantern. As he bent towards the light, Archie opened the door between the rooms.

'Nearly done. Be making the last trip to the well in one minute. Everything's—' He broke off at the sound of a jangle of voices behind him and then Barney's voice said clearly and furiously, 'You bloody fool! Leave him and get back to the boat!' Archie

106

disappeared back into the outer room, clapping to the door behind him.

Josh listened. A mutter of voices but no sounds of a scuffle. So, nothing dire, it seemed. His hand was on the muffler to push it into place when Archie came back in. He thumped the door shut again and pulled the muffler down from his own face the better to say what he had to say.

One look at Archie's face told Josh he had relaxed too soon. Archie was the least impressionable of men. A Chichester man, 50 years old, the press-gang had taken him twenty years ago and he had served eight years in the navy with never a chance to set foot on English soil again until he was discharged at the end of the Peninsular War. Put ashore at Plymouth with an unhealed wound, he had been left like many others, sick or hale, to make his own way home and recover or not as chance would have it.

The brutal conditions he had endured in the navy had hardened him, and though he had never learned to love the navy, what he *had* learned was a pride and a confidence in his seamanship and an aberrant taste for the excitement of war. Coming to settle in Elswick, he had eventually asked Josh to take him into the smuggling band in any capacity Josh was willing to offer, even volunteering what was left of his eight years' pay for a share in the profit or loss of the next run. Josh had never regretted taking him on. Absolutely to be depended on, Josh was aware that Archie regarded him as he had once regarded the naval captains under whom he had served as the keeper of his soul 'under God'. What Josh was seeing now in the man's brown monkey face was a formidable resolution.

Archie said, 'Young Eggles took it on himself to bring in the navy man. The fool thought you'd forgotten him. Barney's sent him off with a flea in his ear. The mischief is, the man – the navy man – saw the last of the goods *and* saw you with your muffler down. He knows you. Swears he'll bear witness to it. He's a midshipman, an officer. These days, the courts will take an officer's word if he swears he saw you and the goods together.'

107

Archie took a step nearer, urgency burning in his face. 'Barney's holding him. He has to be silenced, Josh. Permanently. It's you or him. Maybe the rest of us, too. If you wasn't captain, it would be already done. Give the word and I'll do it yet.'

Captain. To Archie, the man with the right to make decisions. Too easy to say, 'Get it done.' The responsibility was his. He shook his head. 'Send him in here. You and Barney get back to the lugger and make ready to sail. Any sign of trouble put out to sea as fast as you can. If I'm not with you in ten minutes, do it anyway. See you remember.'

Archie nodded, pulled up his muffler and went out. In moments, he was back thrusting a slight figure in midshipman's rig before him. The youngster's hands were still tied behind his back and Josh said, 'Cut him free.'

When Archie hesitated, he snapped, 'Do it.'

When Archie had complied, he nodded and jerked his head towards the door.

With Archie gone, Josh glanced again at his timepiece before looking at the midshipman who was chafing life back into his wrists. Crises that could not be averted were met head-on. One did one's best, or if it could not be avoided, one's worst. It depended on how one looked at it.

The boy was little older than his own eldest son and one whose name he knew. Next to Penn, the midshipmen were the most visible members of the shore-party. They used the village shop and sometimes the inn. They got small welcome, but their money was taken.

'Mr Surtees, isn't it?' Josh asked. Without parade, he took one of the naval pistols from his belt and held it negligently at his side. Surtees' face, already pale, lost all remaining colour, except where a red swelling on his cheekbone evidenced a bruise to come. Stiffly, he nodded.

'It was evil chance you recognized me,' Josh said. 'But foolish of you to be so absolute about bearing witness to it. Perhaps you'd like to think again?'

'No!' Too loud and too quick, the word had been jerked from him with no time for thought. Perhaps because he dared not take it.

'That gives *me* small choice. I've neither the wish nor the intention to spend five years in the navy or seven in jail. And that's not counting the risk of your captain dredging up a reason to see me hanged.'

Dragging his gaze from the pistol, Surtees said with a valiant attempt at defiance, 'Kill me and you can be sure of hanging.'

'Not if you're not around to put a name to me.'

The foolishness of what he had said, brought a momentary flush of colour into Surtees' face. He blinked his eyes several times and Josh guessed that he was fighting the prick of tears. He said, 'How old are you? Sixteen? Seventeen? It's young to turn your back on life, but if your course is set. . . .' He shrugged, half raised the pistol, but allowed it to sink back to his side.

'Because of your age, I'll offer you one last chance, Mr Surtees. Take thought before you answer. How much does delivering me into Penn's hands matter to you? They'll not pin a medal on you for it, so there's not much point to being a hero. Choose right and you'll benefit us both.'

Surtees was too young and unpractised to hide the flicker of hope that first came into his eyes, though he clamped an expression of mulish resistance on his face a moment later. It was to that fleeting hope Josh spoke.

'If you give me your word to forget you saw me, or recognized me, you live. Refuse and make no mistake, you don't leave this hut alive. Give me your word and break it, you're a dead man whatever happens to me because others will see to it. The choice is yours.'

Anguished hope battled despair in Surtees' face before he shook his head in wild denial. 'No!' The word came out in a howl against the temptation to betray his ideals and what the navy expected of him. On a lower note, heavy with the grievous longing of the young for life, he added, '*No. I can't!*'

109

Softly, implacably, Josh said, 'I'm sorry for it, lad. If you've got a family, think of them now and say your prayers. I've no time to spare, so you've one minute only. It will be easier for you if you turn your back.'

The treacherous tears forced themselves forward to glaze Surtees' eyes, but he kept them from falling. He did not turn. From the look on his face, he could not.

The seconds fled by and Josh raised the gun. Cocked it, the snap of metal loud in the silence.

In that moment, the boy broke. With a shamed, inarticulate cry, he dropped his head into his hands, mumbled miserably, 'All right. I'll do it . . . give you my word.'

'You swear it?'

Surtees could only nod.

Slowly, Josh lowered the pistol, uncocked it and tucked it back in his belt. 'Right. Be sure you mean it. What we have to do now, and quickly, is get you back near to your post.'

He eyed the boy narrowly, wondering if he might yet recognize how weak had been the pistol's threat to him: wondering if it would occur to him that he might not yet be out of danger, that he might yet meet a quieter death. But Surtees was deep in the shame of his personal failure, a look of sick humiliation on his face. With no time left now, Josh hoped the boy's unwariness would last long enough to get him away from the bothy quietly and without fuss.

'Your duty officer will be on his way by now, so there's need to hurry,' he said. 'Who is it tonight?'

'Captain Penn. We're short-handed.'

Josh gave a bark of laughter, picked up the lantern and gave the midshipman a slight push towards the door. 'Don't be too hard on yourself, Mr Surtees. Plenty of time yet to prove your worth and win back your self-respect. I'd have chosen as you did. It's one thing to die in a fight, but sheer foolishness to toss your life away for an idea. Dead, you get no second chance.' Deep in his chest, he grunted what might have been another laugh. 'Your luck may change. You and that captain of yours may yet catch me red-handed.'

As they stepped out into the open, he closed the shutter on the lantern. They turned towards the sea. The wind, still blowing landward, carried the clean, salt scent of it. Loosening his knife in its sheath, Josh glanced at the dark shape of the youngster beside him and,putting a hand on his shoulder, drew him closer to walk a little ahead of him. 'Right,' he said. 'Step lively now.'

The tide had turned and the water was choppy now. Barney greeted Josh with surly irritability as he helped haul him into the lugger. The black boat that had brought him to *Sea Dancer*'s side, shot away back to shore to be hurried to her sanctuary by the men who rowed her.

'Another minute and we'd 'uv been gone.' Barney was dour.

'By my reckoning you should be already gone,' Josh said.

Barney ignored that and in heavy silence they set about getting the lugger under way, tacking out into a darkness that was still total. When they were well clear of the land, Barney spoke again. 'What did you do with him?'

No need to say who it was he meant, but there was something in Barney's voice that darkened Josh's already grim mood. 'What d'you think I did?' he demanded sardonically.

'Archie told me. All in a day's work, he said. Navy holds men's lives cheap. Thinks nothing of a death. But Will Uphman heard. Said what the navy did was one thing and if what Archie said was true, he'd no stomach for it and this 'ud be his last trip.' Barney lashed out with his heavy seaman's boot at the base of the foremast by which they stood.

'Did he.' A flat observation, not a question. 'Times are changing, Barney. More will go. For one reason or another.'

'You didn't shoot the boy. We'd have heard.'

'So would the navy,' Josh said drily. That was the essential point that Surtees – too young and too afraid to think clearly – had missed. Equally drily, he asked, 'So what do you think I did?'

The answer, oblique and unhappy, came slowly. 'Well, it was you or him.'

Barney, though no sentimentalist, was a simple man. He stood, a silent demanding presence, waiting, Josh knew, for him to say something that would dissolve his discomfort. But there was a black alien wildness in Josh now that would not allow it.

'Yes . . . it was me or him,' he flung savagely at Barney, and walked away.

CHAPTER ELEVEN

By dawn, news had reached most households in Elswick that there had been a successful run in the area. Right under Penn's nose and, with one exception, without any of the shore-party being aware. An air of jubilant satisfaction pervaded the village which soon made itself felt among the naval men adding to their mortification.

At first light Penn launched a search for contraband in many of the seamen's cottages. For the most part, their womenfolk bore it stoically, met close questioning regarding absent husbands, fathers, sons with dull incomprehension or slyly innocent counter-questions. If the navy did not know why boats were delayed, what kind of seamen were *they*? As for contraband being landed, where was it?

Penn himself accompanied the search-party that went to the Rylands' cottage. The search there was made with scrupulous care for the contents and it was Penn who questioned Prudence Ryland, her eldest son a scowling but silent presence beside her.

Prue answered Penn's questions with a dignified politeness that annoyed Penn almost as much as did her husband's covertly amused way of speaking.

Having failed to trip her into saying anything useful to him, Penn knew he must leave the cottage soon or his mounting irritation would find expression. Yet, with the son of the man who was a constant thorn in his side standing before him, he could not

113

forego demanding, 'And what do *you* know of your father's present activities?'

Freed by the question from his mother's galling prohibition against speech, Andy replied with youthful truculence, 'As much as my mother.'

Penn took a steadying breath. 'Have you no work to go to that you are at home at this hour of the day?'

'I work with and for my father. These days, when he isn't here, I stay home to protect my mother.' He looked at Penn with eyes as blue as his father's, but their expression less under control showed a glitter of fierce defiance as he added, 'The navy's been here before.'

It needed all Penn's self-command not to strike the boy. Turning on his heel, he called to his men and walked out of the cottage.

They had drawn blank everywhere.

Four days later, Josh brought *Sea Dancer* into Elswick harbour on the morning tide. From the time the lugger was sighted, Penn had waited with bitter patience for an immediate search of her to be made. Fish and nothing but fish was found aboard her.

'If I knew what your men hoped to find, I might be able to give them some help,' said Josh, waiting beside Penn on the harbourside. It was deliberate provocation, but there was something about Penn that lured him into mockery.

For a moment Penn could not trust himself to speak, but finding control he said grimly, 'Don't bait me, Ryland. My day will come and then God help you.'

Josh smiled and let it go at that, saying only, 'Meantime, if your men are through, maybe we can get the fish unloaded.'

Nick looked at the young man on the far side of his desk with some curiosity. William Uphman, 20 years old, middle son of old Enoch Uphman one of the Jepsons' boat-building carpenters. Average in height, build and looks and, if you discounted smuggling, an honest enough young man.

114

'I don't understand, Will. It can be little more than an hour ago you came into harbour and now you're here asking me for work. For the past three years, if I'm not mistaken, you have been one of Josh's regular crewmen,' Nick said.

'I'm sailing no more with Josh.'

'Why?'

Uphman looked uncomfortable. 'I'd rather not say, sir.'

'Have you quarrelled with him? Or has he turned you off for some reason?'

'No. It's my own deciding.'

'You must know I have nothing in the sea-faring line to offer you and it's unusual for a seaman to turn to any other kind of work unless forced to.'

'Needing to make a living is reason enough. There are fishermen to spare in Elswick and I've no talent for woodwork like my father.'

Nick nodded. The words rang true.

'Well, I have nothing to offer you immediately, Will, but because the village is so much in need of alternative employment to fishing and smuggling, I am working out a scheme that might interest you. That's if you can afford to wait a week or two. It will be land work and if you put your heart into it there's a strong chance it could give you a good living and a measure of independence before too long. How do you feel about that?'

'I can wait a while, but I can't say I know much about working the land.'

'That can be learnt.' Nick leaned back in his chair looking hard at the young seaman. 'Others will be involved with you, Will. And for that reason, I have to ask you again why you are making this change.'

Uphman took time for thought before saying with a shrug, 'Well, I reckon you'll hear it from someone, so it might as well be from me. You must know we made a run recently. Somebody made a mistake that put Josh in danger. It came down to him or one of the young midshipmen. I guess he had

115

no choice, but taking a knife to a youngster in cold blood is more than I can stomach. If that's the way things are shaping, I want no part of it.'

Nick sat in stunned disbelief for long moments, before he said harshly, 'You're saying Josh killed a young man? A boy?'

'Yes.'

'You saw this?'

'No. But I was by when Archie Nye told Barney. Archie had just left Josh. He said it had to be done. Barney asked Josh about it when he came aboard. All Josh said was *It was him or me.*'

'What happened?'

'We'd had to put the youngster to sleep with a tap on the head first off before we could unload the goods. But at the end of the run, someone took him to where Josh was with a few of the goods that hadn't yet been stowed. The boy saw what there was and recognized Josh who'd uncovered his face. Said he'd witness against him. And held to it.'

It was odd, thought Nick, that though he had never taken part in the trade even as a buyer, Uphman thought nothing of speaking of his smuggling activities to him. As many in the village did. *Josh Ryland's friend.* Was that what they placed their dependence on? Even now when it must be known that friendship no longer existed?

But what right had he to be so shocked? He had killed a man himself when, as Josh had said, it was a case of *him or me. . . .* God help him, he had come close enough to boasting of it to Miss Hilliard and still cringed at the memory. But his victim had been a *man*, armed, and with armed accomplices, and it had happened in the heat and desperation of the moment. Add to that it was with a gun, at a distance . . . if such details could be thought to lessen the enormity of the result. But to kill a youngster with a knife with cold predetermination?

He gave Uphman a date and a time to come again and brought the meeting to a close.

Rising from his chair then, he walked to one of the windows

116

and gazed blindly over the lawns to the sea, brooding in deep disquiet over what he had been told.

How well did he really know Josh? What did he know of his reactions under the pressure of emergency in the course of one of his smuggling runs? Many of the smuggling gangs of Kent and Sussex had reputations for a vicious brutality almost beyond belief. He did not doubt that impelled by circumstances, Josh could kill, as most men could. As he himself had.

It was the cold-bloodedness of the action as Uphman had reported it at which he balked. But lately, Josh had shown himself to be other than Nick had once believed him to be. . . .

But had it happened? *A murder four days old and no word of it in the village?* It was too unlikely. Why should Penn conceal the death of one of his men? *Could* he? What was known was that a sentry had been found unconscious in the early hours of the night the run had taken place.

No, he decided with sudden confidence, no young midshipman had died. Uphman had come to him hot-foot with indignation, giving himself no time to check in the village. But even as his tension slackened, he wondered if he was right.

In Amelia's opinion the eggs sold by the farmer's wife at Twitch-up Farm were the best to be had in Elswick. What she meant was that, at a penny a dozen, they were the cheapest.

Elise had obliged her by walking to the farm for the two dozen for which cook had declared an urgent need. She had just closed the gate of the farm behind her, with care for the eggs carefully disposed in a basket, when she found Mr Mariott coming towards her from the direction of Chichester leading a pale dapple-grey horse limping from a cast shoe.

'Well met, Miss Hilliard. Can I be of help with your basket?' He glanced into it as he spoke and added hastily, 'Oh, no. I am not to be trusted with such fragile merchandise.'

'No, indeed.' She glanced at his horse, said smilingly, 'Last time we met by chance you could not dismount from your horse and

117

this time it appears you cannot mount. Are you frequently so unlucky?'

'No. My unluck is in having the rare occasion come to your attention. But Nimbus here is a well-mannered gentleman, quite unlike Rahu.'

'Nimbus. A cloud. It suits him beautifully and is certainly very different from the other.'

'Rahu is labelled rather than named,' he said drily.

'As Henry has most splendidly labelled his Appaloosa Jupiter. Nothing less than to put him on a par with the lord of heaven and bringer of light would do. It was a kind and thoughtful gift, Mr Mariott. Henry is so very proud of him. But what have you done with Henry himself? With only one more day of his week with you to come after today, I am astonished he has let you out of his sight.'

Looking down at her, it occurred to Nick that her skin looked as attractively clear in the pale sharp sunlight as it did in candle or lamplight. Her hair too, shone with health and cleanliness where it showed beneath the brown straw hat with its cream and tawny ribbons. There came into his mind a recollection of the shimmering, insubstantial vision he had had of her in the early morning a short time ago. . . . It seemed to epitomize the difficulty he had in fixing his perception of her. What was certain was that there was always this tug of an attraction that he did not want to acknowledge, a charm he did not want to see.

He said, 'I had to ride into Bognor on business. But in any case I can't compete with the combined charms of Dotty, Jupiter and young Eddy Hammond. Henry is teaching Dotty to run beside his horse. Or so he thinks. It's fortunate horses and Dalmatians agree so well together. I have yet to tell Henry, but this morning I saw Dotty gripping the end of Jupiter's tail with his teeth and being towed round the paddock with the greatest good nature on the Appaloosa's part. For the sake of Henry's pride in the animal, I can only thank heaven there was no dispute about the game. Appaloosas are not as richly endowed with hair in the mane and tail departments as some.'

'Someone told me that horses, being fastidious animals, accept Dalmatians because they are sweet smelling.'

'It could be so.'

They walked along in comfortable silence for a short distance and then Elise said, 'Everyone is talking of contraband having been recently landed somewhere in the neighbourhood but there seems to be no actual evidence of it. Do you believe it true?'

'Yes.' Short and sharp, barbed with the memory of the keg of brandy John Hammond had found.

'Oh, dear! You sound cross. If it was a misplaced question I apologize.'

'I happen to *know* there was a run and that the goods must have come ashore on my land. I did not sanction it. Knew nothing of it. Will that suffice?'

'I was not prying, Mr Mariott. That there was a run is widely discussed in Elswick and I am as interested as any one else. I could not know that you are better informed than most.'

He stopped, laid a hand on her arm to turn her towards him. 'Miss Hilliard, I am the one who should apologize. It was wrong of me to visit my ill temper on you. At present, smuggling is a subject on which I am out of reason touchy.'

She looked puzzled. 'But if a landing is made anywhere locally it is almost certain to be on your land. Has it not been done before?'

'Of course. My father allowed it and I have not explicitly disallowed it. So, you could say I have no cause to complain.'

Joshua Ryland had not been mentioned, but it was as though he stood beside them wearing his usual slightly amused smile, Elise thought. Was that why Nicholas Mariott looked so bleak?

Nick saw the trouble in her grey eyes and felt an almost overwhelming temptation to kiss her. His hand was still on her arm and involuntarily his hold tightened as though to draw her nearer.

A last minute realization of the foolishness of such an action made him snatch away his hand. Annoyed with himself, annoyed with her for penetrating his defences, he found it easy to find sympathy for the man who had caused her to leave Bath. That combined with the fact that his senses were still answering her attraction raised the treacherous question in his mind, *Approached discreetly, would she. . . ?*

Roughly, he thrust the thought from him. She had given him no cause to suppose that she might. The trouble was he had been celibate too long, he told himself, and saw, with relief, that they had reached Danesfield's gates. Coming to an abrupt halt, he said stiffly, 'I do not care to make Nimbus walk further than he must. Will you excuse me if I part from you here?'

'So close to Greenaleigh as we are, I do not anticipate meeting with any adventure before reaching it.' She dismissed his enquiry lightly, but somehow the humour with which she spoke was thin.

He took the hand she offered him and held it longer than was necessary, thoughts and feelings hopelessly tangled.

'Goodbye.' She disengaged her hand from his, gave him an equivocal smile and walked away. But she had taken only a few steps when she turned and said, 'It can be a mistake to think too much, Mr Mariott. Sometimes the heart is wiser than the head.'

He sensed anger behind her words but she gave him no chance to respond. Turning about again, she walked rapidly away.

Penn's frustration kept him on edge, the thought of being outwitted by a man such as Ryland was a bitter humiliation. Adding to it, was the seemingly unbreakable loyalty of every man, woman and child in Elswick without – or so it appeared – even the suggestion of a threat to make them remain so.

Even among people of better standing he met only a kind of bland reticence. *Ryland?* they said. *A fine seaman. The best.* But too often there were sly smiles, or a guilty shift of the eyes.

Success was necessary for his career's sake, but also for his own deep need. The lesson that he had absorbed was that if Ryland's downfall was to be brought about he, Penn, was going to have to meet cunning with greater cunning. And the sooner he devised a scheme, the better. . . .

One comfort Penn held to himself at this luckless time was his belief that he had made some headway with Miss Hilliard. She seemed to find pleasure in his company and if there was a degree of caution in her expression of it, it was to be expected following the disgrace she had fallen into in Bath. Celia had been unable to discover the precise details of it but was still trying.

It was evening when Josh walked into the Sussex Oak. Ben Saulter came forward to meet him. Anticipating what the inn-keeper wanted to say, Josh told him quietly, 'I'm holding off delivery for a few days, Ben, but all's well. I'll let you know when to expect hand-over.'

'Time enough, Josh. It isn't that, it's Barney.' He ran a hand through his grizzled curly hair. 'He's been here above an hour and he's drunk as David's sow. He's got some gripe against you and he's talking wild. I couldn't shut him up, so I fed him more liquor than he's paid for in the hope of sending him to sleep.'

Josh looked across the room at Barney who was sitting alone at a table, his back to everyone else. From which he judged there was no wilful disloyalty in Barney's behaviour.

'I'll speak to him, Ben. Give me a flagon of your best.'

The ale in his hand, he crossed the room to Barney's table and pushed his way on to the bench on the far side.

Barney looked at him with bloodshot eyes that were slow to focus and late to recognize. When they had done both, he said in a fuddled uncertain voice, 'Damn you, Josh! Damn you to hell! You let me think— You let me think—'

'Well, what did I let you think?'

'—think you'd murdered that boy. Knifed him.'

'I don't order your thoughts, Barney. What you think's your own affair.'

'You *told* me—'

'I told you nothing. You listened to what Nye said and you believed him. Killing the boy was what he recommended me to do.

121

Hell's teeth! he even offered to do it *for* me.' He paused, his blue eyes hard and cold. 'You've known me all your life, yet you found it easy to believe I'd murdered a boy no more than a year older than my Andy. In cold blood. And then you wanted me to soothe your conscience . . . tell you it was all in a day's work. Think about *that*, Barney Tench, and to hell with you, too!' He stood up. Added savagely, 'Open your mouth any wider than you've been doing and you may find yourself on the receiving end of Nye's way of solving problems. If you've any sense left, you'll take yourself home and sleep yourself into a wiser state of mind.'

Picking up his ale, he carried it back to the bar. From there he watched Barney climb to his feet and stumble to the door. Turning to Ben, he said, 'Send the pot-boy after him, Ben, will you? Just to follow behind and see the fool makes it home.'

Lifting his tankard to his mouth, he drank deeply. Not for the first time, he wondered what he would have done if Surtees had not yielded when he did.

CHAPTER TWELVE

The unseasonable mildness of the first week in January gave way to frosty nights and cold, colourless days. On the 19th of the month, a Friday, Will Uphman returned to Danesfield at the appointed time.

'I was wrong about Josh and the midshipman, Mr Mariott,' he said when he once again stood on the other side of Nick's desk. I've seen the boy around and I've learned since that Josh was in a rage with Barney over him believing he'd killed the youngster, which was why he didn't deny it.'

'So you will be returning to your old job?'

The young man gave him a wry look. 'No, sir. Josh would have less reason to overlook my misreading him than Barney doing so. I'd not risk putting it to the test. So it seems I'll have to be a farmer.'

Nick understood. Uphman was young: found the prospect of admitting his error to Josh and perhaps being humiliatingly rebuffed too daunting to his male pride to attempt. He said, 'Then this is what I propose. I'm setting aside one hundred acres of land on the far side of the Chichester–Selsey road to be farmed by a co-operative of twenty. Each man will buy a share at five pounds, the money to go into a central pool to which I will add a sum sufficient to cover the necessary seeds and implements for the first year. You will also pay yourselves from that pool a wage to be agreed among you. If there is a deficiency after harvest in the first year, I will make it up. The co-operative will be self-governed by elected officers – I suggest three – who will meet at regular intervals to decide the general running of what in some ways will be one farm. That's the outline. How do you feel about that?'

'As far as I can see, it seems more than fair to me.'

'That apart then, the land is in good heart. There are twenty acres already put to wheat which is showing well. Thirty acres is at present good meadowland. What animals you choose to rear is your collective decision. There is a standing pig-house, a barn, a hay-barn and available water. The land is valued at twelve pounds an acre and well husbanded should show a clear profit of fifty pounds per annum per share. My farm manager will be on hand to give advice if asked and I shall not ask for rent until the second year. You'll all be working for yourselves, so success or failure will be up to you. Something of the sort has been tried in Suffolk and worked very well, showing profit in the first year.'

He pushed some papers across the desk. 'There's more, but it's all set out here. I know you read, so take that away and study it. If you are happy with it, I shall want you to sign your agreement to its terms. Is there anything you want to ask?'

'My cousin, Thomas, he that's handy man to Mrs Timson, he thinks he might like to join me.'

'Show him the papers then and he can make up his mind. I have three others who have shown interest, one the youngest of a farmer's three sons and needing an outlet with two healthy brothers ahead of him to inherit. A useful man since he knows something of farming. With four or five men enrolled, a start can be made as soon as weather permits. Ben Saulter is putting up a notice in the Sussex Oak so we may hope for more before long.'

By the end of January eight men had signed to join the co-operative, three had wives who were prepared to undertake 'farmer's wife' duties, milking, dairying, attending chickens and whatever else of that nature came their way. They were to be paid twelve pounds a year for their trouble.

124

'You would do better to believe what I say. I am sorry I cannot accept your offer but I wish you well.' She stood up, inclined her head, and walked towards the door. She was half afraid he might attempt to stop her, but he did not.

As she mounted the stairs to her room she became more certain that something had been missing from Robert Penn's declaration. It had been a polished performance apart from that one moment of baffled surprise, but *not*, she was now quite sure, springing from a sincerely felt love.

She could not help but wonder if he knew she was mistress of her own fortune. . . . And perhaps something of the Bath story.

Though the lure of his horse meant that Henry had less time to walk with Elise these days, he was not forgetful of his friend. Elise met Josh Ryland twice more in Henry's company and on the second occasion had been privileged to be shown over the *Sea Dancer*. Not a word had been said about smuggling, but knowledge of the boat's clandestine use was reflected in the occasional amused glance she had turned on him and the blandness of the smile with which each was met.

When she had thanked him for the favour and his time, he had said, 'You're a young lady of spirit, Miss Hilliard. I'd be proud to show you *Sea Dancer*'s paces one day – you and Henry.' The gleam in his blue eyes brightened still further. 'And that's not something I've said to many and never before to a woman, bar Prue.'

A rogue he might be, but his charm was undeniable.

On a day of watery sunshine Elise walked along Shore Lane with Henry and Dotty to the southernmost edge of Elswick. It was late on a Saturday morning, the second in March, and they went to where the lane ended just beyond the Jepsons' boatyard. Past this point the Manor Brook crossed the manor fields into the glebe-lands behind the church to filter through a strip of marshy shore to the sea. There at the limit of their walk, they stood for a while watching the long grey rollers heave sullenly shoreward. Dotty meanwhile, spent an enjoyable, if profitless, time excavating for whatever buried treasure he had in mind before rejoining them. They had turned back towards Greenaleigh when Elise stopped to retie a shoelace, making use of a conveniently placed boulder to do so. Henry however, had glimpsed a recognizable figure ahead leading a horse, and crying, 'Captain! Captain!' raced to meet his uniformed hero.

Alerted by the joyful shout to the presence of a friend, Dotty overtook him and reached Penn first. Not immediately being given the captain's attention, he pawed at Penn's white-stockinged legs, the earth his paws carried leaving grubby marks down their pristine whiteness. Without pausing for thought, Penn brought the crop he was carrying down in a hard thwack across the dog's back. It brought Dotty to a halt with a yelp. For a moment the dog stood in what seemed to be sheer astonishment before his upper lip and muzzle curled away to show every one of his splendid set of teeth in a snarl. It was a very different display from his smile and the deep growl that rumbled up from his chest held clear menace.

Elise had just straightened from her bent position and now hurtled forward as she saw the captain's hand move towards the short sword at his side. In the same moment Henry leapt to grasp the dog's collar and she prayed the boy could hold the animal. Reaching the group, Elise thrust herself between boy and dog and the man.

Penn looked startled by her arrival. Quickly she said, with a glance at the captain's besmirched stockings, 'How very tiresome for you, Captain. I'm afraid Dotty is still young and over-friendly. Henry is doing his best to train him. I'm sure he regrets the damage done.' She turned to Henry. If ever a boy's face reflected the shattering of an idol, Henry's did. 'Henry?' she prompted.

With unconscious dignity, Henry straightened his shoulders, lifted his chin and said with icy courtesy, 'I apologize, sir. The fault

128

is mine that I have not yet taught him to be more' – there was momentary pause as he hunted for a word not yet in his vocabulary, then finished – 'better able to choose.'

The word he had wanted was *discriminating*, Elise suspected, but he had done very well without it.

Penn flushed a dull red and though he raised his hat to Elise, he found nothing to say. He was, she realized, in full dress and was obviously going to a meeting of some importance. Knowing his particularity about the neatness of his appearance, she was a little sorry for him and said placatingly, 'I am sure the mud will brush off when it has dried, Captain.' She gave him a dissimulating smile, gripped Henry's shoulder in warning and steered him quickly away.

She shared something of Henry and Dotty's disillusionment. Whatever the provocation, Penn's response to it had been a savage one.

Late in that same grey, windy month, returning from a uninspiring walk between the gull-haunted, winter-starved fields, Elise went straight to her room. Before she could remove her bonnet there was a knock at the door heralding Henry. She saw at once that he was upset and shutting the door behind him, she said, 'What is it?'

'I—' He gulped unhappily and stared at her wide-eyed.

She reached out to take one of his cold hands in her warmer clasp and drew him across to sit beside her on the bed.

'Take your time,' she said.

'I was tracking,' he said at last. 'You know, like Hawk-eye did in that book you gave me at Christmas, *The Last of the Mohicans*. I'd been reading it again. I saw Andy Ryland ahead of me on Long Lane, so I tracked him.'

'Were you walking or riding?'

'Walking. You need to walk if you're tracking.'

'So Eddie wasn't with you?' Henry shook his head. 'Go on,' Elise told him.

The rest poured out in a troubled rush. He had followed Andy well beyond Danesfield, had seen him constantly looking into the draining ditches that bordered the lane. Presently Andy had stopped, gone down into a ditch and come up with two half-anker tubs roped together in the way smugglers linked them for carrying. As soon as he stood on the lane again, two naval seamen had appeared from behind a hedge on the other side of the lane and were closely followed by Captain Penn. Henry had come up with them to find that Andy was being arrested as a smuggler caught in possession of contraband goods. Andy had protested he knew nothing about the tubs: that a younger boy had told him there was something lying in the ditch along Long Lane that he ought to see.

'Captain Penn didn't seem to listen to what Andy was saying to him,' Henry said. 'He asked Andy where his father was and Andy said he'd ridden into Chichester and wouldn't be back until the end of the day, just before dark. The captain then sent him off with the two seamen.'

Henry looked at Elise with troubled eyes. 'When they had gone the Captain said to me in a hateful sort of way that since I was there I could make myself useful by telling Ryland he'd find his eldest son at the watch-house. He said, "Tell him if he cares to lay claim to the brandy, his son can walk free".'

Elise's feeling against Penn had been hardening with every word Henry spoke. How dared he involve Henry in what looked like a crude trap to catch Josh Ryland with Andy as bait. It was unfair and unkind. A shabby reprisal for his discomfiture caused by that unpleasant little episode with Dotty.

She thought of Joshua Ryland and how he was likely to respond to the situation given his intense love for and pride in his family. That it would be violent, rash and self-sacrificing seemed to her to be more than likely. She suspected that the easy-tempered, toler-ant man could be driven to the far extreme given the right provocation. But how was disaster to be headed off?

Across her silence, Henry put anxiously, 'Can you make

130

Captain Penn let Andy go? Because it's Josh he really wants, isn't it?'

'Yes,' Elise agreed. 'It's Josh he wants.'

'Can you stop him? I don't want Josh caught. I would have asked Uncle Nick to help once, but he isn't friends with Josh any more.'

Nicholas Mariott. . . .

How would he react to knowing what Penn was about? Would he stand by and let the man who had been his friend for close on twenty years be caught in a Machiavellian trap? She needed time to think about it but there was none to spare and the first essential was to lighten the burden laid on Henry's young shoulders. With what confidence she could find, she said, 'I want you to go to your room now, Henry, and try to stop worrying. I am going out to see what I can do and I must hurry because Mr Ryland could be already on his way home. As soon as I return, I promise to come to tell you what, if anything can be done. But no more questions now because there isn't time.'

When the boy had gone she stood for a few moments trying to convince herself that trying to enlist Nicholas Mariott's help had a chance of success. Everything depended on how deep and lasting was the enmity between him and Joshua Ryland now. Did one throw off all loyalty to a friend of long standing when he offended? Who had offended in the first place, she wondered? She recalled the baleful look that had settled on Nicholas Mariott's face when Josh had rejected his offered hand after the storm. There was more to discourage her from making the appeal she intended than otherwise. But since she could see no glimmer of hope in any other direction, to make the attempt must be better than doing nothing at all.

On that conclusion, Elise pulled her cloak about herself and went quietly downstairs.

Walking towards Danesfield, she had time to think of the fact that she was about break a number of social taboos. If she added to that the manner in which she had parted from Mr Mariott the last time she had private speech with him, she could not help but be aware that she was about to lay herself open to repulse.

But then, she thought, reluctant as Nicholas Mariott was ever to think well of her, of what importance could any worsening of his opinion be to her?

CHAPTER THIRTEEN

Landers, the Danesfield butler, admirably concealed whatever surprise he may have felt at Miss Hilliard's unaccompanied visit. As she stepped across the threshold, Nicholas Mariott walked into the hall from the rear of the house. He made no effort to hide *his* surprise.

'Miss Hilliard! Has something happened? Is it Henry?'

She nodded. 'It has to do with Henry, but not Henry alone.'

'Come in here by the fire.' He led her into the bookroom and offered to take her cloak.

'No,' she said, 'don't trouble. I must tell you.' She was more nervous now she was here and the reality of what she was attempting to do was on her. Unaware of the chair in which he was inviting her to sit, she made an effort to subdue her nervousness and said, 'Let me just tell you what has happened.'

'Yes. Go on. I'm listening.' His voice was quiet, kind, his expression attentive.

Quickly and plainly, she told him Henry's tale. He was frowning when she finished and she sensed a withdrawal, not of attention but of goodwill. After a long moment's silence, he asked in a flat voice that boded no good, 'But why have you come to me?'

'Mr Ryland rode into Chichester this morning. He should now be on his way home and I thought you should know what the situation is.'

133

His frown deepened and she sensed that hostility was growing rapidly in him. 'You appear to have shouldered the burden Penn laid on Henry. And I think you are well able to tell Joshua Ryland what has happened, or send a servant to do so, so what is there for me to do?' This was said in a voice devoid of all kindness.

She was sure he guessed what she hoped for from him but clearly he meant to force her to put it into words. Or to retreat. With a pulse in her throat echoing the thump of her heart, she was tempted to do just that. But she would not. With an effort, she said, 'I think you must see what is likely to happen if Mr Ryland goes to see Captain Penn.'

He gave her a grim smile. 'Oh, yes. If Penn poses any real threat to Andy, Josh will kill him. But what is that to me?'

All her hopes were pinned to it meaning *something* to him. That the feeling that had made him offer Josh his hand could still prove greater than the feeling that had sparked the merciless look in his eye when his overture had been rejected.

'I think you would approach Captain Penn with more moderation and gain a better result,' she told him.

'There can be no doubt of it. But again – why I should I interest myself in Ryland's problems?'

His dark eyes, narrowed and glinting, were watching her now as closely as those of a cat waiting for the first flicker of movement from the petrified mouse. There was, too, something in their depth that dared her to say that she knew – or guessed – a good reason. She gathered a last reserve of courage. 'Because now that you know the situation, I think you would never forgive yourself if you don't.'

An unnerving silence followed that. If he had walked out of the room and left her standing there, she would not have been surprised.

At last he said slowly, with chilling contempt, 'By Heavens you balk at nothing, do you, Miss Hilliard?'

She made a small, helpless gesture acknowledging she knew not what. Another moment spent under that inimical regard and she feared her knees would give way.

Unrelenting, he told her, 'You do right to look alarmed. Meddling in matters of which you can know nothing can prove dangerous.' He turned away from her . . . turned back, said with dark malicious humour, 'One point appears to have escaped you, however. Should I attempt to keep Josh from Penn, he would very likely kill *me*.'

Just that one step down from the freezing scorn he had shown her was enough to wrench a nervous, trembling laugh from her.

'Amusing to you, perhaps, but not unimportant to me,' he said drily.

She was thankful that the thread of humour, thin and bitter though it was, still held. But how far dared she test it? 'I agree he might make the attempt.'

'You cannot believe I could hold off Josh Ryland by physical strength, or, indeed, that there is any one man in Elswick who could?'

'By strength alone, no, but—' She came to an uncertain halt.

The glint in his eyes grew sharper. 'Oh, no. Don't run shy now. Let me have the whole of it. But what?'

Still the lighter tone, but no hint of further softening. But what had she left to lose? She said, 'I think you could match and over-match Mr Ryland if you chose. You impressed on me once your ability to cope with sudden danger. Indeed, I have seen you look as—' Again she was stopped by the unwisdom of what she had nearly said.

'Yes, Miss Hilliard? You are in so deep you may as well say it all. How have you seen me look?'

The small saving grace of humour had vanished, his voice had reverted to its former hard and scornful tone. But for that, she might have declined to answer, or perhaps changed what she had been about to say. But stung, she tilted her chin and said the unwise thing. 'Quite murderous.'

He stared at her in astonishment. 'Where, and by what chance did you see such a revealing expression on my face?'

Having gone so far, she dared the rest. 'After the storm when Mr Ryland ignored the hand you held out to him.'

'*You saw—?*' A muscle jerked violently beside his mouth and he swung round and walked a few paces away from her again. A memory revived of Miss Hilliard approaching him, of her chattering breaking in on the overpowering fury of those moments. When he turned back, his hostility was at its peak again and barely under control. In a low, hard voice, he said, 'You are too busy, Miss Hilliard. Take too much on yourself. I see no reason why I should relieve you of the problem. If you find it burdensome, you deserve no less.'

It was a direct attack and she thought now, as she had thought when she had witnessed the incident, how much it mattered to him. How much Joshua Ryland mattered – or *had* mattered? – to him. She had thrust herself into a very private matter and she had expected him to show resentment, but his harshness was having its effect. She said in a shaking voice, 'You may leave me out of the reckoning, Mr Mariott. But besides Mr Ryland let me remind you there are two children to be considered – Andy Ryland and your godson, Henry. Henry is distressed. He not only admires Mr Ryland but regards him as a friend. A friend who makes him laugh. Henry is not over-blessed with friends or opportunities for laughter. And he is over-young to have been dragged into this.'

'I had thought myself one of Henry's few friends. Why did he not come to me himself?'

'He is aware that you and Mr Ryland have quarrelled.'

'As you are. Yet you are here.' He stared at her. Why did he feel so intense a need to punish her? Because she was so damnably observant . . . saw too much!

He swung away from her, stood in thought for several moments before turning back to say, 'Very well. Not for any love of Joshua Ryland, now or in the past, but for Henry's sake, I will attempt to head off Josh and drag Andy from Penn's clutches.'

Something in his expression, the twist of his smile, held her silent. Smoothly, he went on, 'If I am successful, it may appear to

136

you that Ryland benefits. Do not be surprised if he fails to think himself indebted. You are observant beyond the usual, Miss Hilliard, but you do not see or know everything. Take warning that you have sown dragons' teeth today and may find little to your liking in the harvest.'

Words and tone made any thanks she might have offered out of place.

The clock on the mantelshelf striking a few tinkling notes made an opportune interruption. It had proclaimed the last quarter of an hour before four o'clock. From a dry mouth, Elise said, 'It is close to the time Mr Ryland is expected home.'

'Yes. Too close to allow me time to walk you back to Greenaleigh, for which I apologize,' Nick told her, dropping into cool formality. 'I will find someone to go with you.'

'It is only a step. I can very well go alone.'

'So you are always telling me. But it is preferable that you do not.' He crossed to the bell-rope and pulled it. When Landers entered he was given a number of orders, the first of which was to summon Young Pete to escort Miss Hilliard back to Greenaleigh.

Their parting was brief and chilly. Elise said a doubtful 'thank you' and was given a flashing look she could not interpret. Confused, unhappy and deeply weary, she went out into the fading light to join the shyly dumb young undergroom waiting for her.

Her mission had been accomplished, but at greater cost than she had foreseen. . . .

Not many minutes later, his arrangements made – too hurried and too crude for Nick to have any great confidence in them – he went out to where John Hammond stood holding Rahu. The horse had been well exercised that day and, with luck, would be more tolerant of waiting. If however, Josh had returned early, or chose to come by the main Chichester to Selsey road, it was all to no end. Even if Josh came this, the shorter way, inducing him to enter the house was not going to be easy. The fragility, even the absurdity

137

of the plans he had been able to make in the short time available begged failure at every point.

About twenty minutes past the hour as Nick judged, Rahu stopped fidgeting, snorted and pricked his ears. Another horse was approaching. Turning Rahu across the narrow lane, Nick effectively blocked it. It would be a brave hack that attempted to force a way past the Turk.

Josh came unhurriedly into view, riding at ease on his brown cob. There was still enough light for him to recognize who it was obstructed his path.

The cob was drawn to a halt and Nick said at once, 'I have certain news to give you regarding Andy. But not here. In the house.'

A pause, then roughly, Josh said, 'Here will do.'

'In the house or nowhere. Leave it too long and it may be too late. The choice is yours.' Unfair and untrue but necessary.

He was not to know that the last four words roused an unpleasant echo in Josh's head. Not long ago he had used them himself to Surtees. 'Very well.' He turned his horse into Danesfield's drive.

It was Eddie Hammond, summoned from Greenaleigh, who now waited at the end of the drive to take the horses. As the two men entered the hall, Nick indicated the bookroom and followed Josh in. The room was lamplit and John Hammond stood against the wall in which the windows faced the sea. If Josh saw him he gave no sign. A few strides into the room, he stopped, turned, said grimly, '*Now!*'

With equal grimness, Nick said, 'This afternoon Penn set a trap for Andy with a couple of brandy tubs. But the real trap is for you with Andy as bait. Either you claim the tubs as yours, or Andy takes the consequences as a smuggler taken in possession of contraband.'

Josh's stillness presaged storm. 'You wasted time bringing me in here to tell me this?'

'Because here is where you are staying, if you want both Andy and yourself to stay free.'

'*What!*' Josh shook his head in genuine disbelief.

'Penn is waiting for you to charge in on him just as you're set to do, like a bull at a gate. Your boy stands a better chance if I go.'

Under his tan, Josh's natural colour leeched away. 'Oh, no, Nicholas Mariott! I'll see you damned first! I take care of my own!'

'Don't be a fool, Ryland. If you go, you'll either give Penn what he wants or you'll lose your temper. Prue deserves better than to have her eldest son convicted of smuggling and her husband hanged for murder.'

'And you'll make all right? Not while I live!' He glimpsed a movement from Hammond and his eyes narrowed. 'And not you and Hammond together will keep me from Penn.'

'Forget John.'

'You alone?' Josh laughed unpleasantly. 'I could break you in half without trying.'

'Oh, I think you'd have to *try*. Perhaps harder than you think. But I'm not a fool. First you have to reckon with this.' He drew the pistol he had bought in France out of his pocket: percussion and unusual in having a rifled barrel making it far more accurate. Not officially proven yet, but he had proved it for himself in fighting off first Italian and later, Albanian bandits.

Josh dismissed the weapon with contempt. 'I doubt it's even loaded. And if it is, you'd not use it. I know you, Nick. You're soft.' The old name slipped out without his realizing it.

Nick cocked the gun. Extended it. 'You knew the boy I was. Don't trust to that.'

Josh rejected that with a gesture of angry impatience and stepped forward. He had taken two steps only before Nick fired and he was sent lurching back. He attempted another step but his left leg all but collapsed under him. Slowly, unbelievingly, he laid a hand to his thigh, looked down at his reddened palm and then back at Nick. 'God damn you, Nicholas Mariott!' he said with soft violence. 'I swear I'll kill you for this! Andy's my *son*!'

Nick dropped the pistol back into a pocket. It had been a crude solution to a problem but the best that could be managed in the time allowed. 'Be thankful I'm a good enough shot and you have no more than a flesh wound.' He nodded Hammond forward. 'See to him,' he said, 'then get him home. Eddie will lend you a hand and James will be in the hall.'

When the door had closed on him Hammond looked at Josh and nodded with grim satisfaction. 'Mistook your man, didn't you?' He pushed a chair towards him. 'Sit down before you fall down, you great ox, and let me look at the damage.'

'Go to hell!' Josh said.

'In my own time. If you bleed to death, you'll be there before me. It's your choice.'

The words seemed to be haunting him. Held between jagged-edged rage and wounded pride, it was a moment or two before he sat. Then, with the same savagery as he had spoken before, he said, 'I'll live if only to keep my promise to Nicholas Mariott.'

'You're a fool, Josh Ryland. If I were Mr Mariott I'd have let you loose to go to Penn and prove it.'

Josh tried to regain his feet, nearly fell and dropped back on to the chair. Shocked nerves were waking to pain now and he grimaced. 'You don't know what it is to have a son – a boy to be proud of – do you, Hammond?' He wiped a hand over his drawn face. 'Oh, damn it all! I've no quarrel with you, John! Give me a brandy, will you? This is painful enough before you start meddling with it.'

'I've no orders to pamper you.' Hammond's voice was dour. Nevertheless, he crossed to a side table, poured a generous amount into a glass from a decanter and carried it back to Josh. He watched him drink it, then said, 'Now, do the breeches come off, or do I slit them?'

'Slit them. For Christ's sake, leave me some dignity out of today's work.'

140

CHAPTER FOURTEEN

Outside, in last grey glimmering light before night clamped down on the land, Nick again climbed into Rahu's saddle and set him moving quietly down the drive. With Josh out of the way for a time at least, he could spare a moment to consider what he had done and what remained to be done.

But the point on which he found his mind lingering was the fact that he was doing anything at all. Miss Hilliard, disregarding convention, had come to him with some antique idea of undying friendship and her grey eyes luminous with trust that he would adopt Josh's cause as his own. His tardy acceptance of the charge had been made with little charity and uncertain honesty.

As for undying friendship. . . . It was true that once he had thought the bond between Josh Ryland and himself could stand any strain, but he had been wrong. The quarrel that had thrust them apart, seemed to have come out of nowhere. He had no clear recollection of what had been said. Yet from whatever those words had been, had come an enmity which seemed to increase with the passage of time. Remembered offences built into debts; pride demanded their collection. Friendship, like love, could die. *Or be killed.* . . . The fatal stroke had been given to his for Josh when he had walked past him ignoring his offered hand.

In robbing Josh of his right to protect his son he had repaid that offence and more, for Josh's pride burned fiercest where his family was concerned. Memory gave back the cold savagery of

Josh's threat to kill him. It had come from the man's deepest feelings. They stood now so totally opposed, all that was left to them was to find what dark pleasure they could in whatever came of it. As he had told Miss Hilliard.

Walking Rahu towards the watch-house, he had time enough to appreciate the frailty of his position without a legitimate lever with which to prise Andy from Penn's hold. The only possibility he could see was to oppose Penn's bluff with bluff.

It was wry comfort to reflect that win or lose ultimately the price he would be called on to pay would be the same.

Expecting Joshua Ryland to come to his lure, Captain Penn had no pleasure in seeing Nicholas Mariott standing on the far side of the table that served him as a desk.

Nick said starkly, 'I will come straight to the point, Captain. I am here to secure the release of Andrew Ryland whom I believe you to be holding on a false charge.'

Damn his arrogance! Penn regarded him with cold dislike. He had risen to his feet when Mariott had entered; now he sat down with the briefest of gestures towards the second chair, a gesture that was ignored. Penn took time to bring his temper under control before saying, 'Well, that is certainly to the point, Mr Mariott. But why should you think so? And what rights do you have in the matter? As you yourself told me, the Rylands are not your tenants and report has it that you are no longer a friend of the family.'

'My rights are those of any man who sees injustice to do what he can to avert it. As to why I think the charge against Andrew is false, it appears to me a little too convenient that the boy should receive a message to the effect that he will find something to interest him on Long Lane and that you should be waiting there for him to find it.'

'Events do occasionally fall out conveniently.'

'Rather more than that in this case. A convenience by which you hope to exchange the son for his father.'

142

'If the father claims the contraband to be his and his son merely there by chance, I shall consider exchanging the lesser rogue for the greater.'

'Baiting a trap with a man's son does not trouble you?'

'Where rogues are concerned, no. But I am not required to justify my actions to you, Mr Mariott.'

Nick waited long enough to isolate his next words. 'You will know who Admiral Lavinger is, I'm sure?'

Penn's eyes narrowed suspiciously at the seeming irrelevance. 'I've heard of him, of course. A power at the Admiralty.'

'Quite so. An uncle of mine with whom I am on good terms. If you know anything of his reputation, you will know that he is a stickler for honesty and would not turn a blind eye to a naval officer using dubious means even in pursuit of his duty. Nor, let me remind you, would Captain McCulloch. If either heard a suggestion that an officer's motivation was less than irreproachable, a shadow would undoubtedly fall on that officer's reputation.'

Unwarily, Penn snapped, 'What motive could I have other than to catch a known villain?'

'Ambition, Captain? A boost to your career? Promotion is not easy to achieve while the country is at peace.'

Penn knew he was right. The Admiralty would not look askance at ambition used to promote the navy's interests, but doubt of an officer's motivation could place a long-lived question mark over his worth. A darker hostility flared into his face, but holding still to his temper, he said, 'I do not care what you choose to think, Mr Mariott. If Ryland confesses, it is unlikely there will be a lengthy examination of either the means by which he was brought to do so, or the motives promoting those means.'

'Even given a hostile witness?'

'But you were *not* a witness.'

'Still, I think I would be heard. And though you might achieve your main aim, doubt of the purity of your motive could be created. And would be remembered, as you must know.'

A nerve jumped in Penn's cheek. Damn the man! Standing over

him in judgement in all the security of his position as a prosperous landowner; a security for which he had never had to struggle. He looked away, staring angrily at the now black square of the unshuttered window. 'What do you want?' he asked harshly at last. When he looked back at Nick, his loathing was undisguised.

'I think you would be wise to reconsider the evidence against Andrew Ryland and decide it is too circumstantial to be safe.'

It took a long moment before Penn could speak and even then he could not keep the grinding of envy and resentment out of his voice. 'How pure are *your* motives, Mr Mariott? You are reputed to have no connection with the smugglers, yet whenever I get close to one, there you are to save his skin. It would take no more than two men of standing, you and Sir Roland let us say, to swear to Ryland being the smugglers' ringleader and that would put an end to his activities.'

'Twice, and twice only I have intervened when you have been on the wrong tack. As for Josh Ryland, catch him with contraband fairly and squarely and I shall not lift a finger to interfere, I assure you. But I will not swear away his freedom or any other man's for convenience's sake whether mine or yours.'

There was silence broken only by the flames tearing at the coals of the small fire in the grate. Deeply grudging, unwilling now to meet Nick's eyes, Penn said, 'I'll see to it you hold to those words. For now, you may take the boy.' His chair grated back over the wooden boards. Going to the door of the room he gave an order to one of his men. A minute or two later, Andy came in, blinking in the lamplight as though he had been kept in the dark. Tense and wary, his gaze swung between Penn and Nick. But when Penn barked 'You may go,' he was young enough to show his infinite relief.

It was black night when Nick and the boy left the watch-house. A thin, whining wind had risen, blowing in from the sea now, pushing heavy banks of cloud before it and bearing a hint of rain to come. Nick, leading Rahu, sensed the questions pouring through

144

Andy's mind as they walked out of the field into Shore Lane, but the silence between them held over the short distance to where a footpath to Josh's cottage led out of the lane. There, as they paused, Andy, awkwardly abrupt, asked, 'Where's my father?'

Why had Josh not come? was what he was really asking. Nick said, 'He had a small accident which prevented him coming. Nothing to worry about.'

The next question would have been 'But why *you?*' and he had no intention of answering that. By now, Hammond should have got Josh home: let him tell his son whatever he chose. Forestalling further questions, he went on, 'Better get home, Andy. Your parents will be anxious. Goodnight.'

Leading Rahu, he walked rapidly away into the darkness. The words faint on the wind, he heard Andy fling 'thank you' after him. He doubted the boy would repeat his thanks after he had seen Josh.

Now he had leisure to mull over what had passed between himself and Penn and to wonder what Admiral Lavinger would have to say should he ever learn that someone quite unknown to him, had claimed him as his uncle. . . .

Her mind in turmoil, Elise took refuge in her bedroom soon after reaching Greenaleigh House. With leisure to savour to the full all the unpleasantness her appeal to Nicholas Mariott had brought down on her, she sat on her bed and wondered at her own fool-hardiness. She had thought she could endure whatever expression Nicholas Mariott gave to his justifiable resentment of the assump-tions she had made. But the stinging whiplash of his words and manner had cut through all her defences to her cringing spirit. What had made it so much worse was being so sure that to no other woman would he have spoken so roughly. It had been personal.

She had known for some time that he was attracted to her: knew, too, that he resisted the attraction with fierce determina-tion. There was no room left in her mind for doubt that he had

145

heard the Bath scandal and judged her by what he had heard.

She drew what consolation she could from the fact that in the end he had taken on the task of saving Andy from Penn and Josh Ryland from himself. So perhaps if she had not been entirely right in her surmises, she had not been entirely wrong.

As her nerves quietened she realized that the cold and hurried way in which she and Nicholas Mariott had parted had not allowed her to ask to be informed of the outcome of his intercession on Andy Ryland's behalf. But was he likely to agree to send her news?

When Betty came in to help her change for dinner, her lips were pursed and there was a gleam in her eye and a look on her face closer to one she had sometimes worn as Elise's nurse than to the one she wore as abigail to Miss Hilliard.

'What have you been doing, Miss Elise, that Master Henry's young groom should come asking me to pass a message to you?' she demanded.

Elise's face lit. 'Did he? Oh, good! Tell me what he said.'

'I don't know that I ought. What have you to do with grooms and messages and such?'

'Nothing at all. I haven't seen or spoken to Eddie all day. It will be to do with Henry and something he saw while he was out this afternoon, but I can't tell you anything about it, it is a secret between Henry and myself. Now do be quick . . . tell me what he said.'

'Hmm.' Betty could see no cause for concern there and she relaxed. 'Well, all he said was to tell you that "Andy is home".'

'Excellent! Something like that is just what I wanted to hear.'

Betty, behind her now and beginning to unbutton Elise's day-gown, said dourly, 'Master Henry hasn't been getting into mischief, has he?'

'No. The poor boy has very little opportunity for it.'

She whisked herself out of Betty's hands as soon as she could and hurried to Henry's room to give him the good news and to tell him that it was his godfather who had achieved the success.

Immensely cheered by the information, Henry said hopefully,

146

'Perhaps he and Josh will be friends again now.'

A reasonable hope, but in the light of what Nicholas Mariott had said to her, not one Elise felt she could place much faith in. 'Perhaps,' she said.

The mere fact of knowing that Andy Ryland was free did not satisfy Elise for long. Now she longed to know how it had been done and by what means Joshua Ryland's objections to relinquishing responsibility had been overcome. At the first opportunity she questioned Eddie who was embarrassed to have to tell her that he had given Uncle John his word to do no more than pass on the message she had received and say nothing to *anyone* of anything he had seen or heard at Danesfield this day.

It was more than a week after her own visit to Danesfield before Elise saw Mr Mariott again and then it was after Sunday-morning service.

With some ingenuity she avoided drawing attention to her manoeuvring, and managed to intercept him before he left the churchyard. Surrounded as they were by people, neither time nor place allowed anything but a direct approach. In a low, hurried voice, she said, 'Mr Mariott, I must speak with you. Could you – *would* you contrive to walk with us as far as Greenaleigh?'

He gave her a gleaming look. 'Your cousin Amelia will not welcome me as an addition to your group. She would prefer you to invite Captain Penn, I am sure.'

'I did not mean— I should have said walk with *me*. I should like – *need* to speak privately with you.'

'Dear me. Is this wise, Miss Hilliard? To walk apart in full view of all Elswick's chief gossips?' The tone was teasing but there was an edge to it that matched the glint in his eye.

'Oh, do please be sensible. You must *know* what I wish to speak about.'

'Yes. Unfortunately I suspect I do. And sorry as I am to disappoint you—'

'We are leaving, Elise,' Amelia said, with a brief nod for Nick as she, with Matthew and Henry drew level.

147

'Yes. I will follow in just a minute,' Elise said, her gaze fixed pleadingly on Nick.

'I will see Miss Hilliard home,' Nick said after a pause.

The Woodstows passed on and Nick gestured towards the gate. 'Shall we?'

'Thank you. Indeed, I do thank you.' Elise began to move with him.

'You have no occasion to do so, because I do not mean to satisfy your curiosity, Miss Hilliard.'

'Oh.' The bluntness of that held her silent for several moments. Then, hopefully, in a small voice she asked, 'I beg your pardon. But in the circumstances, have I not a small right to know?'

'As I see it, not even a small right.'

Deeply mortified, there was a long pause before she ventured, 'I know you think me very interfering, but—' Glimpsing his expression, her courage and her voice expired together.

'Your *buts* have a lot to answer for,' Nick said grimly.

'Well, Mr Ryland did not kill you, as you expected. That much I can see, though I begin to be sorry for it,' she said with spirit.

That amused him enough to trip him into saying with sly mildness, 'Whatever may have been his initial intention, I'm afraid I frustrated his design by shooting him first. You may have noticed he was not in church this morning though *Sea Dancer* is in harbour.'

She stopped walking and turned to put a delaying hand on his arm. '*You did not!* No, of course you did not!'

'Indeed, I did.' And then because the temptation was irresistible, he added with unctuous reassurance, 'Do not be concerned, the body is buried under my cellar floor and my servants are too well trained to talk.'

She snatched her hand from his sleeve and turned away, colour flaring into her cheeks. 'You are still determined to punish me for coming to you, and you may be happy in knowing that it is quite as chastening as you mean it to be.'

Following an infinitesimal pause, he said, 'Very well, I will admit

148

CHAPTER FIFTEEN

The Colbrookes' house was not large and their evening parties were limited by the fact that their rooms could not comfortably accommodate more than twelve people at a time and dancing was not possible. The party they gave at the end of the first week of April included Matthew and Amelia Woodstow and Elise. There were no surprises among the other guests and familiarity allowed an agreeable ease of communication. Hearing the rise of busy voices in the drawing-room where they first gathered, Elise smiled at her own amusement that people who saw each other so frequently could still find so much to say to one another.

Alexander Rivardeau was her dinner partner and remained more than usually attentive to her afterwards. So much so that in the end she made an excuse to leave the room. Walking through the nearest door she entered a narrow passage from which two or three more doors opened. One stood ajar showing a faint light. She was hesitating at the threshold when someone else came into the passage and walking quickly, reached around her to push the door wider open. Involuntarily, she stepped forward into what appeared to be a small study. It was lit only by the glow of a dying fire. When she turned she was facing Captain Penn.

He said urgently, 'I must talk to you.'

She glanced at the door he had carefully closed and moved sideways out of line with him.

'Please hear me,' he said again. And then pleadingly, '*Please.*'

151

She stood still. Said with annoyance 'Captain, if you are about to renew the offer you made me before, I beg you will not.'

'But I must. I love you. Want only to marry you. Will make you happy, I swear. Believe what I say.'

Words that had been missing from his first proposal, but spoken now, did not ring true. But beyond that, could he believe that his behaviour to Henry's dog and to Henry himself could have no influence on her?

She said with cold firmness, 'As I told you before, Captain, I have no wish to marry. Not you, or anyone else.'

He stepped nearer and grasping her by the upper arms, gave her a small shake. He had nursed the hope of marrying her so long, it now meant too much to him to relinquish it easily. Just the possibility of losing the security her fortune would give him shook him out of his usual common sense. 'You cannot mean it. Let me show you—' He pulled her close, bent his head to bring his lips down hard on hers in a fierce demanding kiss.

Thoroughly angry, she wrenched her head aside. 'How dare you! Let me go!'

He did not. Instead, he shook her again and harder. It was a poor way to woo a woman but he had endured too many frustrations recently and fear of losing the prize he coveted broke his control.

'Damn you! You led me on. Made me think— You cannot back away now.' His anger flared higher, driving him into greater error. 'If you marry me you will at least achieve respectability!' he told her furiously.

'Respectability, Captain?' Elise pounced on the give-away word.

Penn saw the abyss and tried to draw back. 'I mean I can't offer you a fortune, but marriage is a more respectable state for a woman than spinsterhood.'

'I think the truth, Captain, is that you cannot offer me a fortune, but *mine* has an attraction for you.'

'Oh, damn you! Damn you! What are you but a hussy who was found out. Fair game for any man. Undeserving of an offer of marriage!' He dragged her back into his arms and this time the kiss he fastened on her mouth was brutal. He freed a hand to roam her body in a way that was a violation. She fought him fiercely but to little effect against his easy strength.

She was freed so suddenly she almost fell. Neither she nor Penn had heard Nick Mariott come into the room. He had torn Penn away from her with a violence that pitched him into the nearest wall and knocked him to the ground. Taking a long threatening stride towards Penn as the man gathered his wits and rose, Nick waited, his hands fisted, wanting – *needing* – an outlet for an over-powering anger. Only a last minute recollection of how unpardonable it would be not only to brawl in the elderly Colbrookes' home, but to make Elise Hilliard the centre of attention, held him back. When Penn was on his feet, he said bitingly, 'Get out!'

Penn shot a furious look from him to Elise, curled his lip and said, 'If that's your taste, you're welcome to her.' He strode to the door and went out slamming it shut behind him.

Nick turned to the girl. She looked to be on the brink of tears that only determination was holding back, but then her head bowed and she shook it as though in protest.

Nick had walked in on Penn's words, '. . . *a hussy who was found out. Fair game for any man!'* Infuriated to see her struggling in Penn's arms, he did not pause to consider the justice of the man's words but took immediate action.

'Are you all right?' he asked, stiffly, because, for some reason, his anger was already switching from Penn to her. Miss Hilliard, it seemed to him, exposed herself to trouble and censure at every turn.

But realizing then how much she was trembling, he was unexpectedly touched. Without thinking, he reached out and pulled her into an embrace that was entirely directed towards comforting her. For a moment she stood rigid, but realizing there was no hint of constraint in his hold, that it offered only kindness, she relaxed and bowed her head against his shoulder as if in utter weariness of spirit.

He sensed that tears were falling now, but her trembling eased. He found himself patting her back and murmuring the kind of consolation one might give a child. Gradually he became aware of other things, of the scent of her hair which smelt sweetly, as though recently washed and rinsed in flower-scented water; of the warmth of her skin which came through the thin silk of her gown and the delicacy of the body he was holding. Feelings assailed him that in relation to this particular woman were not new and never welcome, but were now stronger than ever. They were feelings decidedly inappropriate in a man who has just rescued her from another man's mauling.

Putting her at arms' length, he said, 'He must have frightened you, but you are safe now.'

Her head lifted sharply and her grey eyes were wide with outrage. 'He did not *frighten* me – he disgusted me! I feel—' She made a small sound of repugnance and left the sentence unfinished.

The outrage she had expressed was more in keeping with the Miss Hilliard he thought he knew. So hardy a spirit could need no further reassurance from him. One of the several causes for being angry with her rose up in his mind. Unwisely he gave voice to it. 'It was not advisable, I think, for you to be alone in here with Penn . . . indeed, with any man.'

She moved sharply away from him. Looking at him coldly, a small, bitter smile turning her lips. 'Yes, of course, Mr Mariott. I alone am to blame, am I not? That deepens my debt to you for coming to my rescue. Perhaps you should have left me to learn a needed lesson.'

She gave him a small mocking curtsy, walked past him and out of the room.

He stood for long moments fighting a flood of anger that seemed inexhaustible. It had been the sound of raised and recognizable voices that had drawn him into the room and wild as his rage against Penn had been, it had not lessened when turned on Miss Hilliard for having got herself into an awkward situation.

154

Now, in the last moments, some of his anger was directed at himself –or the misplaced wave of tenderness he had felt for her. But in the end the focus of his fury was again Elise Hilliard for being who she was and what she was.

He took a deep breath. It was time to master his feelings and endure the remainder of the evening with what grace he could find.

Keeping country hours, the Colbrookes' party broke up at 10.30. Nick was among the first to leave. Still irritable from the events of the evening and needing to be alone, he walked away from the house very briskly to avoid having to accompany any of the other guests even part of the way. From the time of his intervention between Penn and Miss Hilliard, the evening had been awkward and unsatisfactory. There were too few people present to easily conceal a sudden disunity between three of them. Had the Colbrookes noticed and wondered at a certain loss of harmony among their guests?

Drawing level with the small gate into the copse, impatience decided him to take the short cut through it to the stableyard. The light from a half-grown moon was increasingly fitful as clouds drifted in from the sea, but the trees were not yet in leaf and he was well acquainted with the path.

As he came through the last of the trees, he heard Dotty's mellow but imperative barking. The sound was distant, as though the dog was still shut in the house. The Dalmatian was not a noisy dog, he rarely barked and never without good cause. Nick frowned, wondering what was making him do so now. As he reached the stableyard, Rahu neighed, loudly and angrily. The moon was veiled again, but his eyes were sufficiently adjusted to what light there was for him to see that the Turkoman's door was minutely ajar. Now too, even though muffled by straw, he could hear the horse's unquiet trampling and the occasional thud of an irascible hoof against the wooden inner panelling. Someone was in his box and since there was no light, it was unlikely to be either Hammond or Young Pete. Pulling the door wide, Nick stepped in.

155

In the confines of the loose-box, it was black night. Rahu, he sensed, was at the far end, close to his manger.

'Gently, Rahu. Gently,' he said, letting the animal hear a familiar voice.

Immediately, there was movement off to his left and he demanded, 'Who's there?'

The answer came not in words but in a rush of movement and he found himself wrestling with the intruder. Groping for a hold, he found a throat and grasped it. Occupied though he was, he heard the hurry of footsteps across the yard and was aware of the swing of a pendent light advancing and retreating. His assailant was also aware. Nick heard a snorting, indrawn breath and in the next moment felt what seemed like a heavy blow just above his heart.

There seemed no interval between that and opening his eyes to a changed scene. He was lying on straw on the floor of a loose box that was not Rahu's. There was folded cloth under his head and a clean horse blanket laid over him. Two lanterns hung from a beam showing Young Pete standing beside him with John Hammond who was kneeling. On his other side stood Andy Ryland.

Looking across at the boy, John was saying in a more brutal tone than Nick had ever before heard him use, '. . . and if he dies I'll see you hang for it!'

Nick tried to speak but no sound came. He tried again, whispered, 'John . . . what happened?'

Hammond's head turned sharply to look down at him, his expression desperately anxious. 'Young Ryland. He stuck a knife in you.'

'He shot my father.' The boy's voice was pitched high above its normal level, but there was nothing self-excusing in it. He was simply giving what to him was sufficient reason. And then he said again with a boy's mounting frustration, 'He shot my father. And Pa won't tell me – he won't *tell* me!'

No, Nick thought, Josh would not want to tell the boy about

what he would only see as his own failure. He attempted to sit up, or thought he did. Nothing happened except a small hiss of sound forced from him by the excruciating pain that shot through him. He waited for the pain to ebb a little then turned his gaze on John and asked faintly, 'How bad?'

'Beyond my skill, Mr Mariott. I've done what I could, but Sam footman's gone for the doctor. You've lost a lot of blood. Now, somehow, we must get you to your bed.' He looked towards Andy, adding venomously, 'And get the constable for *him*.'

'No.' Had he said it aloud? Nick tried again. 'Wait.' Every word was an effort and there was a rolling tide of darkness waiting to reclaim him. He laid desperate hold on consciousness. What he wanted to say was important. 'Not Andy.' He sweated with effort. 'Unknown assailant . . . John . . . that's an order.'

John wrestled visibly with a hunger for revenge. Conceded unwillingly, 'If you will have it so. But it's wrong and if anything happens to you, I *will* see him hang!'

Nick wanted to shake his head but could not. With painful effort he gathered what strength he could find for speech.

'Andy . . . listen.' The boy's blue eyes, so like Josh's, met his. In them, Nick read defiance, fear and something that might have been anxiety. 'Does Josh . . . know . . . about this?'

'*No!*' Andy's voice rose again. As though, with the blindness of the young to consequences, it had not occurred to him that Josh would ever learn of it.

With sweating effort, Nick said again, 'Listen. . . . Josh must not know. *Must not!* For his sake. Not yours . . . not mine. Swear to it.'

Andy looked bewildered.

With no strength left, Nick said imploringly, '*John. . . .*'

'Since it's what he wants, swear to it, you bloody young savage, or I'll break your neck here and now!' John cried furiously.

'All right. All right. I swear.'

'Send . . . him . . . home.' With the last sighing words, Nick let go and slid thankfully into the waiting darkness.

157

Pain woke him briefly when he was lifted on to whatever they had found to carry him. And it was pain that woke him again some time later in a bed and a room he knew to be his own. Bending over him, was Doctor Fenton who had attended his father in his last illness. It was his cleansing of the wound, gentle though it was, that had brought him awake.

'Yes, Mr Mariott,' the doctor said, as though Nick had spoken, 'very uncomfortable, but I will soon be finished.'

The underestimated discomfort continued, but at last, bandaged and nightgowned, Nick lay unmolested. Dr Fenton held a glass to his lips with the command 'Drink.' He did and was told, 'You'll sleep now.'

While waiting for that happy release, he heard Fenton say, 'I'll stay the rest of the night, if you can accommodate me.'

'Of course, sir.' That was Landers' voice. And then there was John's asking, 'He'll be all right?'

'I can give no promises yet. A knife's rarely a clean weapon, but he's young and healthy and all that is possible I shall do.'

'And so will I.' That was John again. Truculently positive. No one contradicted him.

Nick smiled inwardly. A groom in the master's bedroom and Landers uncomplaining . . . it was his last thought before sleep overtook him.

CHAPTER SIXTEEN

The following morning, as Elise walked away from the village shop, she met Lady Anstey.

'Oh, Miss Hilliard! Doom! Doom indeed, has fallen on us! Have you heard?' was that lady's greeting.

Elise repressed a smile and looking suitably interested, said, 'Indeed no. I've heard nothing alarming.'

'Mr Mariott. . . . Last night after leaving the Colbrookes' house he was struck down in his own stableyard. A man with a knife. Can you believe it? And now dying, they say. So terrible!'

Shock held Elise motionless, her mind pulsing with protest against belief.

Miss Hilliard's silence, her stunned expression, were all the encouragement Lady Anstey needed and she babbled on, 'The man escaped before the grooms could apprehend him. A stranger, it is believed. So dreadful! Who is safe? What times we live in!' Having begun her tale with its climax, she found herself unable to lengthen it. She patted Elise's arm. 'You must be careful in your rambling, my dear. Take a groom with you and do not go too far. Though if we are to be attacked here in Elswick, *where* is safe?' She walked on, looking about her for the next person to whom she could impart her news of disaster leaving Elise trying to bring her chaotic thoughts under control.

A stranger, Lady Anstey had said; certainly anyone in Elswick would have recognized Joshua Ryland had it been him. But what motive could a stranger have to kill Nicholas Mariott?

She felt physically sick and desperate to know more: to know that Lady Anstey was mistaken or had exaggerated and that Nicholas Mariott was not dying. She did not pause to wonder why it was so vitally important to her, she simply accepted that it was and turned her mind to the quickest way of discovering the truth. The most direct was to go to Danesfield and enquire: but going there on behalf of others was one thing, putting her interest on public display by doing so on her own behalf would not only be embarrassing to herself but to Mr Mariott – if he survived.

She had not moved since Lady Anstey had left her. Now, looking around a little dazedly as though the world must have changed in the last few minutes, her unquiet gaze reached the nearby church. Though it would be imprudent for her to call at Danesfield, it was not so for everyone. If Mary knew of the attack, as a long-time friend and as the vicar's deputy, she could quite properly make enquiry. She or her father might have done so already.

Mary was at home but had not yet heard the story. Her father, she said, had gone into Selsey very early to speak to the vicar there on some church matter.

When told what Lady Anstey had said, Mary was almost as shocked at Elise. 'Nicholas attacked and thought to be dying! Oh, no! Poor Nicholas! Why would anyone—? Can it be true?'

'Lady Anstey appeared certain, but—' Elise shook her head doubtfully. 'But something must have happened. An enquiry at Danesfield would settle it. I should like to do that because Mr Mariott recently did me a great kindness, but it might occasion remark if I did so,' Elise said. In saying that Nicholas Mariott had done her a kindness she was aware of having stretched truth to its limit. What Nicholas Mariott had done had not been for her, nor done in kindness But at this moment that had no importance for her.

'Well, I certainly may do so. Nicholas and I have been friends since childhood as everyone knows. Will you come with me?'

This met Elise's wishes completely and, very thankfully, she agreed.

They went without delay and it was only in the short interval between Mary sounding the knocker and the door being opened that Elise felt again the fullness of dread of what they might discover.

She was aware of Mary asking to see Mrs Duncan and taking a grip on her senses, she followed her into the drawing-room, where the housekeeper soon came to them.

'Is it true that Mr Mariott has been attacked and badly hurt?' Mary asked at once.

Elise held her breath.

'All too true!' said Mrs Duncan with worried indignation. 'He came across an intruder in the stables last night and the man stabbed him. We are all quite dreadfully upset.'

'But he *is* alive? Will live?'

'He's alive, yes, but out of his senses and so weak from loss of blood! Nor is there any certainty of his survival yet. Dr Fenton remained with him all night. He has gone now but will return before long.' She shrugged helplessly. 'Oh, Miss Staunton! I cannot believe it has happened. If it had not been for the timely arrival of Hammond and Young Pete, the villain might have struck again and finished the master there and then. And because it was obvious how badly Mr Mariott was hurt, the men were too busy caring for him to pursue his assailant who made off when they arrived. But who in Elswick could possibly want to kill him? It must have been a stranger, as the grooms said.'

There was one man who had declared his intention to do just that, Elise thought, and Nicholas Mariott had believed him.

Mrs Duncan could add little more to what she had told them so far and, declining refreshment, the two young women left the troubled household.

Elise found the days that followed hard to endure. There had been no comfort to be derived from the uncertain report of Nicholas Mariott Mrs Duncan had given them and it was frustrating to be unable to make follow-up enquiries in her own right. Not wanting to expose the depth of her interest even to Mary, she made shameless use of Henry. It was only proper, she told the boy, that he should enquire as to his godfather's progress when he went to take Dotty for a run, which he must be sure to do every day since no one else would have time to do it. Henry, shocked and upset by what had happened to Uncle Nick, was more than willing to do both, but even his reports were too beggarly to satisfy Elise while they contained any uncertainty regarding his godfather's survival. Her only other recourse was to implore an uncommunicative Heaven to be merciful.

Rarely fully conscious, Nick alternately sweated and shivered through several days and nights. Passing from uncharted intervals of pain and nightmare to black oblivion and back again, it was Dr Fenton's attentions to his wound that roused him to a clearer awareness at some time on the fifth day.

'So you are back with us, Mr Mariott,' the doctor said in a satisfied way. 'The infection in your wound that gave you a fever is almost conquered. It is always a danger with a knife wound. A bullet is cleaner. However, if you are obedient to my instructions, you should make a good recover now.'

'How long. . . ?' The whispering voice seemed not to belong to him.

'That we shall see. If you are going to fret over matters of business you will only slow the process. Be wise, take the Bible's advice and possess your soul in patience. Impatience could result in your yet leaving worldly affairs behind forever.'

Sheer bodily weakness allowed Nick little choice but to accept what the doctor said. There were longer periods of sleep now, but even those were not always quiet. He found it difficult to separate night from day, sleeping from waking, actuality from opium-induced nightmare. Danger seemed to stalk among the shadowed images . . . Josh . . . himself . . . pursuer and pursued. But who was which was never clearly decided.

162

As his body healed, his mind returned frequently to what he remembered had happened from the time he had heard Dotty barking until he was lifted into his bed. He recalled his anxiety to keep Andy from suffering the consequences of his action; remembered his anxiety to conceal it from Josh. Why had it appeared so important? Something to be saved against the day of reckoning? Because unknowingly, Andy had delivered into Nick's hands, a weapon against which his father had no defence.

If, perhaps *when*, he chose to use his knowledge. The black thought hung in his mind, part of the nightmare. *Hatred . . . the longest pleasure. . . .*

Until his present dependency, Nick had not felt the need of a valet, but to his surprise, John Hammond made a neat-handed stand-in for whose services he was exceedingly grateful. He spent long hours in the sickroom without neglecting the care of horses and stables, and was ready to point out to anyone who might have questioned his competence to manage both roles, that he had trained Young Pete himself and he could be trusted to maintain efficiency.

The strength of Hammond's indignation over what had happened was, in a way, a measure of his loyalty. It was a loyalty that surprised Nick. He would have been equally surprised to learn the degree of popularity he had with others he employed and with the majority of the villagers.

Hammond's anger against the Rylands, father and eldest son, simmered on undiminished through the days of Nick's recovery until he felt Nick was strong enough to hear him voice it. When Nick brushed aside his opening complaint, he said roughly, 'No, sir, I *don't* understand. He may be young, but he came to do murder.'

'No, John. I think he came with no very clear idea of what he wanted.'

'He came with a knife and he used it. The intent to murder was there.'

'Most fishermen carry knives. They need them all the time. I suspect it was in Andy's belt when he went into the loose box. Rahu probably frightened him and that was when he drew it. Rahu would have kicked him into the next world if the boy had got any closer to him. You know that.'

'The point is, it was *you* he used the knife on.'

'He panicked when he heard you and Young Pete coming. He just struck out blindly. It was too dark to see in the loose box.'

'Shape it how you will, sir, the long and short of it is, he damned near killed you!'

'An unlucky hit. I had him by the throat and big though he is, the boy's only fifteen.'

'Old enough to hang, so the law says.'

'You surprise me, John. I had no idea you were so vengeful.'

'Where there's reason. Josh and his son were already obligated to you and I don't understand their ingratitude. Now young Ryland owes you his life and to my mind, Josh ought to know it, too.'

Nick shook his head. 'Some debts carry too high a rate of interest. Leave it, John, because I cannot explain it to you.'

'No. Well. . . . I'm wrong to argue with you, Mr Mariott, I know. But I hold to what I said before, young Andy is lucky you're still alive, because I'd have seen him hanged if you wasn't.'

'I hope you would not, knowing it was against my wish. And I am, after all, still here.'

'No thanks to the Rylands, father or son.'

'What I find odd, John, is why the boy did not run when he had the chance.'

There was a long pause before Hammond said unwillingly, 'I don't know.'

'Did he help you move me out of Rahu's box?'

Hammond scowled. Even more unwillingly, he said, 'Yes.'

Nick nodded as though the answer had confirmed something for him. 'Forget it, now, John, and be sure you and Young Pete tell no one the truth of the matter. It is important to me, so I ask you to remember it.'

He shook his head at his groom's look of frustration and said, 'John, I owe you my life. I know that it is not by luck alone that I am alive. Doctor Fenton told me that it was the speed with which you sent for him and what you did for me before he arrived that went furthest to saving my life. Believe me, I'm more than grateful to you. And I'll put up with a little argument from you now and then. But not on the subject of Andy Ryland.'

Praise embarrassed Hammond into silence, made him restless, and before long, he thought of something that called him away.

Two weeks from the time he was struck down, Nick reached the stage of convalescence when, lying in bed, he felt rested and well enough to be up and about, yet when out of bed and doing no more than sitting in a chair, he found himself physically weak and querulous with impatience because of it. Condemned to rest on his bed for an hour after lunch, as he was now doing, his mind remained determinedly clear and active. Nothing to do but read or think. On this particular day, finding something was nudging at his mind for attention, he let it in.

It had to do with his conversation with John. For the first time he allowed himself to recognize that from the time Josh had ignored his outstretched hand and walked past him with the two Dutchmen after the storm his attitude to him had been divided: dealing directly with him it was conscious and alienated; but any threat to Josh from others found him acting from deep instinct in his defence.

He let memory take him back to the beginning of his association with Josh, to his lonely boyhood when he had hung about the harbour admiring the sloop Josh had owned at that time. To this day, he remembered the explosion of pride and pleasure he had experienced when Josh had offered him friendship. Remembered, too, the man's steady fulfilment of that role through all the years that followed. Seen in the light of his own present maturity, it was a remarkable constancy shown towards a child who had no natural claim on him, the more remarkable because Josh had been no more than 22 years old at the beginning. He, Nick, had desperately needed that friendship. It was Josh who had shown interest in his boyish concerns, who had built up his self-confidence and given him rough and ready guidance towards manhood. All things his father had failed to provide.

Recalling the suddenness with which the quarrel that had divided them had arisen, he wondered if it was the ripening of his confidence in the years he had been absent from Elswick that had brought it about. Had he remained in Elswick, Josh would have accepted the change in him as it happened. But he had returned from his travels fully fledged and through his father's death, had become within a few months the largest landowner in the neighbourhood and a man of some importance in and to the village. Accepting responsibility, he had taken a stand opposed to Josh's in the matter of smuggling, declared his intention of accommodating the navy on his land and asked Josh to abandon his chosen way of life. Had the transformation of his protégé into a man of authority been too sudden for Josh to accept? Had the *imperator* that was an essential part of the man's character been unbearably affronted?

With better understanding, Nick thought, he might have salvaged something from their friendship. He had not inherited his father's noisy, tempestuous and often physically demonstrated temper: his temper was his own and when roused found expression in quietly spoken, cold, cutting words which, perhaps, had their own kind of cruelty.

Injured pride had caused him to cherish the idea that he hated Josh, when what he really hated was the withdrawal of a friendship he valued and the unyielding antagonism that had replaced it.

He could acknowledge now that he owed Josh far more than the man's present wilful intransigence could wipe out. With that done he felt as though a burden had been lifted from him. A moment later, a self-deriding spurt of laughter shook him. Unless Josh reached a similar understanding, what happened between them in the future was likely to prove one-sided and might well

166

prove no laughing matter for himself.

He turned, then, to considering other less than successful relationships. His half-hearted pursuit of Miss Rivardeau was one. Neither he nor the lady had made a long-lasting impression on the other, it seemed. As beautiful as she was, as unvaryingly well mannered, amusing, conversable, in the end, her sameness wearied. He wanted something more than a beautiful doll as a lifetime's companion. What did *she* want? Not Nicholas Mariott, he was certain. Now that he thought about it, it struck him that there was about her the easiness of a contented woman; a woman who, perhaps, had within her the satisfaction of emotions fully absorbed and reciprocated. If that were so, who was the well-beloved and where was he? Not in Elswick he was sure. Perhaps one day they would all learn.

When Miss Hilliard slid into his mind his new-found clarity of perception deserted him. Miss Hilliard set up a turbulence that made it impossible to think of her without attendant irritation. She was a breaker of rules . . . a rebel. A quiet one, perhaps, but like all rebels she created disorder. In fact, if he traced Andy's attack on him back to first cause, he could fairly say it was through her agency he had been struck down. The sum of the matter was that Elise Hilliard bedevilled him too thoroughly for him to make any concession towards her. . . .

CHAPTER SEVENTEEN

It was not until Nicholas Mariott was known to be out of danger and set firmly on the road to recovery that Elise allowed herself to think about the extent of her concern for him and what it implied. Her anxiety had gone well beyond what she might have expected to feel for an acquaintance and not by any stretch of the imagination could she call him a friend. Could she even say she liked him?

To realize now, fully, painfully, that what she felt for him was much stronger than mere liking, that in fact she loved him, was, in a way, humiliating. She had a keen eye and cool head – or so she had always thought. So by what roundabout route had she come to this irrational state of loving where there was immovable prejudice that shut off all hope of return?

She could not even claim that he had given her cause to love him; though Heaven knew he had given her cause enough to heartily dislike him. In such a witless condition as she found herself, common sense suggested she put herself as far as possible from the chance of further folly and that as soon as possible.

May had come in with a burst of fine warm weather that soon graced hedgerow, meadow and fruit tree with a fine display of bloom and blossom. *Sea Dancer* and one or two of the larger yawls and ketches sailed off in hope of reaping a harvest of mackerel off the north coast of Cornwall if the expected shoals were running as they should be. Elswick could now show an innocent face to the world as though no thought of illegal trading had ever crossed the mind of any among its inhabitants.

Twice in those first blossom-wreathed weeks, Elise saw Mary Staunton in the distance walking with the stranger Mary had danced with at the Ansteys' last party. And then one day, turning a corner past the smithy, she met the two face to face. There was a moment's startled, slightly embarrassed silence before recovery began and Mary introduced her companion as an old acquaintance, Edwin Linstead. Mr Linstead, she said, had recently been appointed to a living in a village near Petersfield.

They remained chatting for a minute or two and when they parted, Elise was left with the impression of the same glow about Mary as when she had seen them dancing together. The following day Mary sent a note to Greenaleigh House inviting Elise to take tea with her that afternoon.

When she arrived, she found Mary in a state of unusual nervousness, her hands restless, half her sentences left unfinished. At last the tea-cups rattled into silence and almond biscuits, having been tardily remembered and dispensed, Mary looked at Elise and said tensely, 'I want to tell you something . . . ask . . . need your advice.'

Elise smiled encouragingly. 'Tell me. Ask me.'

She began slowly, uncertainly, before getting into the flow of her story. 'We met first – that is, Edwin and I, met six years ago. My father was unwell for some months and Edwin was sent as curate to help him. He had not long been ordained. He lived with us while here and we . . . we fell in love. He wanted to marry me. Papa would not hear of it. He said Edwin was too young, had no home to offer me and being without anyone to promote his interests, had poor prospects. He said – he said Edwin was presumptuous and sent him away. Told me to forget him.'

She sat looking into distance for a moment before continuing, 'I could not forget him. And he did not forget me. We wrote to each other. Not often because I did not want Papa to discover it. I know it was wrong, but—' She shook her head helplessly. 'It has

169

been six long years but now Edwin has been given a living, has a home to offer and has come to find me. He enlisted the help of Lady Anstey. You know how romantically minded she is. And it *was – is –* romantic, because when we met, we knew that nothing had altered.'

Mary lapsed into silence again and Elise prompted, 'So now?'

'We still want to marry.' She looked pleadingly at Elise. 'I should not burden you with this, but there is no one else . . . no one I would rather consult.'

'It is no burden. If I can help, you know I will. Tell me what the difficulty is.'

'As before, it is my father. He has settled firmly into the belief that at twenty-six, I am past the age for marriage. And in a way, he has become dependent on me. I think he . . . I am sure he will be angry. Because it is Edwin. Because it will disrupt his routine.'

That last most of all, Elise thought. She said robustly, 'You are far from being too old to marry. And your father is not an old man, Mary.' That he was a very selfish one could not be said. 'He will adjust. He is an attractive man, not too old himself to marry again. You have a right to take the happiness offered you. The right to marry and have a home of your own. As he did when he married your mother. You are of an age to marry without permission and my advice to you is not to ask for it. Simply tell your father you are getting married and ask for his blessing. With or without it, hold firm. If you and Mr Linstead approach him together you will be support for one another.'

'Yes. Yes, of course. I see that is the thing to do. But oh, I wish I were as brave as you.'

Elise laughed. 'You do not know how cowardly I can be. But you were brave enough to write to Mr Linstead against prohibition. You will find all the courage you need for Edwin's sake whatever your father says or does.'

Mary looked at her and smiled. 'You said that as though you truly believe it. I'm so glad you came to Elswick.'

Returning the smile a little ruefully, Elise wished she could be as glad to have done so. Wished that courage was all that was needed to change the way Nicholas Mariott regarded her. She said, 'Not the most desirable mentor perhaps, but do as Lady Macbeth advised her husband, "Screw your courage to the sticking-place, and you'll not fail".'

'No. You're right. I must not. Shall not.' Though her smile was less certain now, Mary spoke firmly.

Love and marriage seemed to be in the air.

Two days later, Irma Rivardeau, for once without her brother, called to see Elise to propose a walk. They had gone no more than far enough to be where no one could observe them when Irma brought them both to a halt.

'Miss Hilliard . . . Elise . . . I cannot wait – I must ask you, do you feel anything at all for my brother?'

Elise found no quick answer to the abrupt and extraordinary question and Irma hurried on, 'He is very much in love with you, but I know him to be afflicted by a quite unreasonable self-distrust. He does not realize, cannot believe in his own attractiveness. *You*, I am sure, must see it. Feel it.' Her amber eyes fixed on Elise, demanding agreement.

'Certainly I am aware Mr Rivardeau is an attractive young man,' Elise agreed slowly. 'But I have not been aware of his having such regard for myself as you suggest.'

'But he does! And *you* – do you not feel something for him? You must do!'

Elise regarded her with astonishment. Irma was making what amounted to a proposal by proxy. 'I am sorry to contradict you, Miss Rivardeau. I like your brother, but I do not love him. And if he loves me as you think, surely he would tell me so himself?'

Irma shook her head. 'No. It is as I say, Alex is disabled by his deeper feelings. Cannot express himself. It is because I am anxious for his happiness that I have come to you. He does not know that I am doing so, of course, and I rely on your good nature not to tell him. But let me add to that how delighted I would be to have you

171

for a sister and beg you to give it serious consideration.'

'It is not possible.' Elise's tone was sharp. 'And I beg you not to give him any encouragement to pursue the matter himself. Please let no more be said on the subject.'

Something close to hostility blazed for a moment from Irma's amber eyes, but she turned away with a small deprecatory movement of one hand. 'Now I have vexed you and for that I am sorry. Only concern for my brother's happiness would have made me dare so much.'

There was too much embarrassment on both sides for the walk to continue and by mutual agreement it was abandoned.

The incident confirmed Elise in the opinion that it was past time to leave Elswick. It was too small a place for the knots and snarls of relationships between those frequently thrown together to go unremarked. She found herself envying Mary the certainty of an attachment that had endured unmoved through six years of separation, even though it still had some difficulty to overcome. No period of waiting was going to be rewarded by any change to the dislike and disapproval with which Nicholas Mariott viewed her. She remembered with aching poignancy those moments of what had surely been tenderness when he held her in his arms after Penn's assault on her. Had they been real, or had she simply imagined them? Perhaps read more than was there into a sympathy he would have shown any woman in distress?

By the third week in May, Nick was able to resume his normal life except for a three months' ban on heavy lifting and over-vigorous exercise. He responded to the proposal of a week's visit from an old friend with enthusiasm and James Kefford arrived a few days later.

They had met at Oxford and found themselves kindred spirits. Chance had brought them together for a time in Italy and they had kept in touch since. James was now Lord Kefford and in possession of a comfortable estate in Wiltshire.

Living at a distance, James had heard nothing about the attack

172

on Nick but he was quick to catch the attitude of watchful care that surrounded him at Danesfield and remarked upon it.

'Your servants all seem to look on you as though recently returned from the brink of the grave,' he said. 'Have you been ill?'

'In a way, yes,' Nick said, and reluctantly gave him the briefest outline of what had happened.

'And you have no idea who?'

'No.'

James glanced sharply at him. 'You were never a good liar, Nick. I scent a mystery.'

'And a mystery it will remain.'

'Ah. So you do know who. A jealous husband perhaps? What have you been up to?' He met Nick's frowning look with a wide smile and an uplifted hand. 'No. *Pax vobis!* I do not mean to press you. Keep your mystery.'

The hint of a lord at Danesfield brought a spate of invitations. The Ansteys, restless at the knowledge of how long it was since their last ball, had already given notice of their next and to this Nick was committed. It fell within the period of James's stay and consulted, he was happy to accept the invitation Lady Anstey quickly extended to include him.

A lively, pleasant-looking young man with manners to match, he was assured of instant popularity which suffered only a slight decrease among the younger ladies when it was learned he was already married.

The usual welcoming warmth and gaiety of the Ansteys' parties had embraced the two men when they entered the drawing-room. Dancing had already begun and James's gaze roved with interest over the dancers until his attention was caught by one in particular.

Looking where his friend looked, Nick laughed. 'Still an eye for the prettiest women, James? You're looking at one of the latest of Elswick's in-comers. Very beautiful and still unmarried.'

'Oh, yes . . . very beautiful,' James said, the odd expression on his face reflected in the dryness of his tone. 'I met Miss Rivardeau

173

and her brother a year or so ago when they were in Tonbridge and Elizabeth and I were visiting my grandmother there. He caught Nick's look of enquiry. 'Not taken your fancy, has she, Nick?'

Nick shook his head. 'Only briefly.'

'Just as well. Be warned – she never looks beyond her brother. And for your ear alone, she is looking to marry him to a fortune and set up a happy *ménage à trois.*'

'Good God!'

With a small cynical laugh, James said, 'I don't think the Almighty would be in any way concerned in it. But there it is. These things happen.'

It was not the only revelation James Kefford had for Nick that evening,though for a time there were too many people eager for an introduction to his lordship for further conversation between them. They were together again, however, when James, looking across the crowded room, exclaimed, 'By all that's holy – *Elise!* So this is where she disappeared to! Excuse me, Nick, Miss Hilliard's acquaintance is one I don't choose to neglect.'

Nick watched his swift passage across the room to Elise Hilliard's side and saw the pleasure with which they greeted each other. Before long they had joined the dancers and Nick found himself watching their laughing animation with a crabbed discontent for which he had no rational explanation. She had kept her distance from him since she had left him in Harrison Colbrooke's study with that cutting rebuke. It seemed to him that whenever he encountered Miss Hilliard he was doomed to show a clumsiness, even a churlishness of manner that afflicted him at no other time. As he had acknowledged before, she threw him off balance,but what excuse was that?

It was some time before James came back to him again and when he did he was still bubbling over with the pleasure the meeting had given him.

'Elise tells me you know each other. She's a great girl, isn't she? Damn shame what happened to her in Bath. She had no need to hide herself away though. That was her great-aunt's doing, of course. Silly woman, Tabitha Hilliard, though I suppose one should make allowances. A spinster, as ancient as the hills and senile with it. Those who knew Elise had a pretty good idea what had happened, and a number of her friends, myself among them, suggested to the gentleman concerned that he'd be better off a long way from Bath and France would not be too far. Unfortunately, Elise had disappeared by that time and her great-aunt swore she did not know where. Whether she did or not could never be pushed beyond doubt. As far gone in years as she is, it was impossible to press her as one might wish as she is always ready to dissolve into hysterical tears.'

He glanced at Nick's unrevealing face and said, 'I imagine you know something of this since you're almost one of the family. The Woodstows I mean. I seem to remember you stood godfather to poor Charles Woodstow's boy.'

'I've heard nothing beyond something young Henry let slip about a scandal being the reason for Miss Hilliard leaving Bath,' Nick said woodenly.

'A scandal deliberately created by a needy and unscrupulous young man to get his hands on her fortune. He arranged matters in such a way as to force her into marriage with him or face ruin. I believe there was the thought – perhaps even the attempt – to rape her to achieve his ends. If so, he met his match in Elise Hilliard. She foiled him on that count and preferred facing the scandal the rest caused to being married to a scoundrel. It was the weak-minded bleating of Tabitha Hilliard that drove Elise away under a misguided sense of obligation because the woman offered her a home when her parents were killed.'

'Is Miss Hilliard's fortune so great?'

'Her parents left her fifteen thousand pounds. Enough to keep her in reasonable comfort. What is not known to everyone is that her godfather left her considerably more. To those who do know, her fortune is great enough to be a temptation to any fortune-hunter on the look-out for an heiress. I tell you, Nick, if I were not a happily married man, I'd be well pleased if Elise would consent to marry *me*. And not for any reason to do with her fortune: she's a diamond of the first water.'

Nick heard him with feelings too mixed to distinguish one from another, but which gradually resolved into a strong impression of having been cheated. Very early in his acquaintance with Elise Hilliard he had sensed her quality, her innate honesty, but would not give it the credence it deserved. For reasons that now appeared inadequate, he had preferred to preserve the preconception of her character that Henry's unsupported tale had raised in him. Because he had been angered to find himself attracted to her? He had, he knew, looked for fault in everything she did . . . and still could not escape the power her charm exerted over his senses.

But it went beyond charm; it was the essential nature of Elise Hilliard that held him fast. Too late he was forced into recognition of how much more he felt for her. Too late because it seemed to him there would be something shabby in approaching her at this eleventh hour simply because he was now better informed. His gaze followed her as though it could not leave her. She was wearing a yellowish dress, a warm colour close to apricot. The gown's silk flowed over her delicate curves outlining them, and stronger than ever he felt the pull of a desire that could never know satisfaction.

He remembered the indignant pride with which she had corrected his idea that Penn had frightened her, saying, *He did not frighten me – he disgusted me!*

At this moment, Nick disgusted himself. If he was cheated, he alone was responsible.

CHAPTER EIGHTEEN

Elise's meeting with James Kefford had given her a great deal of pleasure. He had cheered her with his report of her friends' active support, had expressed their wishes and his own for her early return to Bath. In amusing addition, he had given her an account of the latest tittle-tattle in that city. She had needed to know that her friends had stood firm and were eager to welcome her back.

The evening had been all the more comfortable, too, when she discovered that Nicholas Mariott was not dancing, which averted any chance of his again noticeably failing to dance with her, or doing so to their mutual unease. She had kept as far from him as circumstances allowed and was relieved he made no effort to seek her out.

Her return to Bath, however, suffered another deferment. Mary was engaged to be married. The vicar, faced with two determined people, had coldly and reluctantly agreed not only to bless them but to marry them. The wedding was to take place in the middle of June. Under Mary's gentle pleading, Elise had given way and agreed to support her through the ceremony.

Sea Dancer and her companions returned at the end of May. Josh and two other skippers had sold their plentiful haul of mackerel before their return and had netted high prices. There was jubilation among the many who shared the financial rewards of a successful expedition.

Henry was in awe of the amount Josh's catch was reputed to have fetched. 'Nearly a thousand pounds!' he told Elise. And with a small boy's pride in being knowledgeable, went on, 'Josh told me how what the fish fetches is divided. Half goes to the upkeep of the boat, then two shares go to the captain, one share to each of the crew and a half share to the ship's boy. That would be Andy this time. Then there's the landsmen . . . those are the men who scrub out *Sea Dancer*'s hold and generally look after her while she's in harbour, or beached, or anchored off shore. They get a quarter share each. So you see, the bigger the catch and the better the price, the more everyone gets.'

'I suppose the upkeep of the boat costs quite a lot,' Elise said doubtfully, thinking over the allotments.

'Oh yes. There's the harbour dues. Spars get broken. Sails shred in a bad storm. Cables break. Ropes and things have to be replaced. Josh says they're all expensive. And sometimes the boat itself gets damaged. And there's always barnacles,' Henry finished darkly, with all the wisdom of a little learning.

The news of Mary Staunton's engagement was all the more interesting to the village by reason of the surprise it caused. How had the romance come about when no one had known anything about it? If Lady Anstey was to be believed, she was the single exception. That was generally discounted as few could believe that her ladyship could possibly have held her tongue over such an interesting piece of news. But over the short period of time it had been in her possession, she had managed it. Buoyed up by being, as she felt, central to the occasion, Lady Anstey also undertook to dragoon the vicar into giving his daughter an engagement party, offering herself as hostess. Meanwhile, escorted by the vicarage gardener who sometimes drove the vicarage gig, Elise and Mary went to Chichester to shop for bridal clothes.

The engagement party, at the vicar's insistence was to be at the vicarage: a quiet, dignified dinner-party suited to an engagement of a young woman past her first youth . . . and, of course, suiting him. The house did not lend itself to a large number of guests, or to dancing, and sixteen was the most the vicarage dining-table could seat comfortably. With Edwin Linstead, his brother and his wife to include, the nine places that remained after the Stauntons and Ansteys, limited the choice of guests. Elise as future brides-maid had to be invited and the vicar felt it would not be right to omit Matthew and Amelia Woodstow. Mr Mariott was too impor-tant to be left out, as were the Colbrookes. Mrs Timson was an old friend and her nephew and niece were invited to keep a balance between the older and younger generations.

Though Lady Anstey was disappointed not to be allowed to have the party at the more spacious manor-house, all went well as parties under her management seemed always to do. It was a talent perfected through many happy repetitions. Even the vicar unbent under its benign influence and managed to speak to his future son-in-law for fifteen untroubled minutes before the evening ended and before he remembered that the man was causing a major upheaval in the even flow of his home life.

Because the evening was successful, it was late when it ended. Most of the guests had said their goodbyes and left when Mary asked Elise to come to her bedroom to see her wedding gown which had arrived from the Chichester dressmaker that after-noon. Elise looked around for the Woodstows, but the vicar had drawn Matthew into his study to see a book he had recently acquired, a French account of the history of the Norman conquest of England by Thierry, first published two years previ-ously. They shared an interest in medieval customs and institutions and would no doubt have fallen into a discussion last-ing past midnight but for Amelia hovering with ill-concealed impatience nearby. Elise estimated she had enough time to look at the gown and followed Mary upstairs.

Elise had been with Mary when her choice was made and was pleased to see that the cream silk and pale violet trimmings had made up into a gown simple enough to content Mary's anxious modesty and pretty enough to satisfy herself and perhaps please

179

Edwin Linstead. She said what would keep Mary happy in her choice but lingered only long enough to admire the bonnet that matched the gown before saying she must not keep her cousins waiting.

They had reached the top of the stairs leading down to the hall when a servant admitted a late newcomer. Until this new arrival, there had been only two people in the hall, Nick Mariott and Sir Roland. Recognizing Captain Penn's voice, an instinct she could not have explained made Elise stop and hold back Mary.

'Forgive this intrusion,' Captain Penn was saying, 'I am here only for the briefest moment.'

'I will call the vicar,' Sir Roland said.

'Do not trouble him, sir. My business is with you and is no more than to inform you as a matter of courtesy of the possible use of weapons within the area of your magistracy.'

'Whatever is happening, man?' Sir Roland asked alarmed.

'Late today, information I had received earlier regarding contraband goods being landed in the neighbourhood on tonight's high tide was confirmed. It allowed enough time to send for a small detail of marines, a promised reinforcement for my own men. They should be arriving before too long and I hope that the reception we shall together give the smugglers will put an end to their rascality once and for all.'

There was a long moment's silence, then Sir Roland said stiffly, 'It is good of you to let me know what is happening, but I trust you will remember that if the men are local, they are likely to be simple villagers unused to carrying weapons.'

'Perhaps not as simple as you think, sir, since they have long been successful in evading the law. And perhaps not as weaponless as you suppose.'

His gaze travelled past the magistrate to reach Nick. 'I have your word remember, Mr Mariott,' he said obliquely, and under the cold, thin tone rang a note of triumph.

That is why he came! The thought exploded in Elise's mind. Not to see Sir Roland, but to ensure Nicholas Mariott knows what is to happen and is in some way made impotent by whatever pledge he had given Penn.

But she had made some incautious sound which caught the captain's attention. There was mockery in the slight inclination of the head he directed at the two girls before turning away towards the door. Unaware of Elise and Mary who were now descending the stairs, Sir Roland asked Nick bluntly, 'What the devil did the man mean by that last remark?'

'For some reason he is convinced I am in league with Joshua Ryland and would warn him of an impending ambush if I knew of it. We crossed swords when he laid a trap for Josh using Andy as bait. It was then I said that if he caught Josh fairly, I would not interfere.'

'Would you not, Nick? *Will* you not? I do not know what lies between you, but you were good friends for many a year.'

'I gave Penn my word and I will keep it.'

'Well, if he brings off Ryland's capture, I for one will be damned sorry to see him caged. And there are the other men of the village to be thought of.'

'Josh and they know the penalties for what they do and will have only themselves to blame.'

'You're damned severe in your judgements, Nick. May you never find yourself—' He broke off as Elise and Mary reached the bottom of the stairs.

The vicar, too, accompanied by the Woodstows and Lady Anstey came into the hall now and there was general bustle as coats and shawls were brought and goodbyes said. Elise took a long covert look at Nicholas Mariott. They had said nothing to each other in the course of the evening that courtesy did not require, had hidden their feelings behind carefully controlled faces. At this moment though, his expression, less under command, was grim and she saw that it cost him some effort to attend to those who spoke to him. Whether the emotion with which he wrestled was anger with Penn or with Joshua Ryland she could not be sure. But that he would keep his word to Penn she did not doubt. Nor

181

that he would pay a price for it however hard he tried to deceive himself.

Walking with her cousins down the vicarage path, she was already debating the wild idea that had leapt into her mind. If she adopted it, there was every possibility of disgrace and even of danger resulting, and with no certainty of success at the end. Added hazards were the shortage of time and the means by which it might be done. On one point alone she was clear: she knew now why she was considering ignoring every tenet of her upbringing to take action that she shrank from. It was not for Henry, or Joshua Ryland, or anyone else but for Nicholas Mariott alone. And recognizing that, the decision to attempt it was decided, with the wry reflection that if ever he learned of it, her reward would be a greater contempt than she had yet earned from him.

Amelia set the pace for the quarter of a mile walk from the vicarage to Greenaleigh House and it seemed to Elise it had never taken longer. She was thankful that because of the lateness of the hour they retired to their rooms as soon as they reached the house. In the privacy of hers, Elise hurriedly changed into serviceable shoes and replaced her silk shawl with a dark jacket. Blowing out her candle, she emerged cautiously from her bedroom, checked there was a light under the Woodstows' door and turned to her right.

Sliding a hand along the wall for guidance, she went quickly and carefully along the passage to the servants' stair and on down to the kitchen region. There was no light there and passing all the service rooms, she felt her way to where a door opened into the stableyard and drew the bolts. Crossing the yard, she mounted the wooden steps that led to the grooms' quarters above the stable and knocked as loudly and persistently as she dared on the door there.

It seemed an age before there was any sound within, but at last a muffled, muttering voice made response. Her heart was hammering and her throat had dried and it seemed an age before the door opened. Just able to identify the shadowy figure standing inside, without preliminary, she demanded, 'Eddie, will the cob carry me?'

'Miss Hilliard! Is it really you?' Eddie peered through the gloom.

'No time for questions, Eddie. If Brown Boy will carry me, will you come down and saddle him? Be quiet and don't bring a light.'

She turned and hurried down again without waiting for his reply. His bewildered voice whispered after her, 'Be down quick as maybe, miss.'

He had boots and breeches on and was shrugging into a jacket when he joined her.

'What you up to, miss? There's no side-saddle for you and I can go anywhere you want.'

'No, it is something I must do. Your own saddle must serve. And do please be quick!'

Troubled though he was, her urgency persuaded him and he did what she asked, though he muttered a bitter litany of complaint while doing it. 'I don't like it. It can't be right, surely! 'Tisn't safe! Can't see why I can't do whatever 'tis you're about.'

'There would be more danger to you than to me, so please don't argue.'

Eddie held his tongue after that, except for a glum, 'I suppose you *can* ride.' But even his silence was weighted with protest. Very soon the cob was ready to lead out into the yard.

Taking the reins from him, Elise said, 'Will you help me up?'

He did it quickly and neatly, with a gulp for the just discernible view of a silk-clad leg exposed to the knee despite her fairly full skirts. 'You'll be black and blue tomorrow,' he told her.

'Never mind. I don't expect to go far, nor to be long. If things go wrong though, you have not seen me, did not hear me take the horse. Remember it, Eddie, please. Go back to bed and don't come down again tonight. I'll see to Brown Boy.'

She walked the cob quietly down the short drive, then set him along Long Lane as fast as the darkness allowed, bouncing unpleasantly in the saddle until she recaptured the rhythm. If Josh Ryland was landing a cargo anywhere near Penn's area of surveillance, it would have to be somewhere towards Sidlesham and Pagham. *Surely.* . . . she added to herself, in the hopeful Sussex way that was both a question and a reassurance.

Her nerves tightened and tightened as the cob carried her through the night. She had asked Matthew a seemingly idle question about today's tides as they walked back from the vicarage. If what he said was right, high tide was *now*, but she reached and passed Twitch-up Farm without any sign of the smugglers. Between listening fearfully for sounds of Penn's men ahead or behind her and trying to pierce the darkness past the dark bulk of the hedges and fields towards the sea to her right, she was beginning to despair. She must be coming to the end of Penn's area of surveillance and might soon be into that of another and unknown shore-party. Suppose she had passed the landing place in the dark? She had to get closer to the sea.

The barest suggestion of an entrance to a narrow path between hedges going in the right direction made her check Brown Boy and turn him into it. The encroaching growth made it so narrow a tunnel that before she had gone far she was forced to dismount and lead the cob who soon began to show his dislike of the clutching briars and slapping branchlets. Between his balking and the constant ruinous snagging of her garments, she feared the sound of their passage must alert anyone nearby. The sudden harsh, unsettling cry of a nightbird set her nerves even further on edge and when a moment later she walked into what seemed darkness made solid, she gasped aloud.

At once a hand was clasped across her mouth, she was grappled to rough clothing and Brown Boy's reins wrenched out of her hands.

CHAPTER NINETEEN

With easy strength, Elise's captor swung her round and half carrying, half propelling her, took her forward in the direction she had been going. The man must have managed to loop Brown Boy's reins over an arm because the cob followed on, still jerking and blowing with annoyance at the night's tribulations.

The path ended at a small swing gate that gave entrance to a field which they crossed close to the nearby boundary hedge until reaching a larger open gateway into another field. There, sensed as much as seen, Elise was aware of other figures near at hand, of the quiet mutter of men's voices, an impression of busy-ness. The voice of her captor growled in her ear, 'No noise, or it'll be the last sound you make.' The hand across her mouth was removed. 'Now,' said the voice. 'Who're you and what're you doing here?'

She was not in the hands of naval seamen or marines she realized with relief: she had found the smugglers. Recovering some hardihood, she returned, 'Never mind my name. My business is with Mr Ryland. It's desperately urgent. Tell him Captain Penn is on the way with a detachment of marines and do hurry.'

Her voice, her assurance, and her message, together carried enough conviction to make him release her and turn to grasp the arm of one of the nearest men and say, 'Get Josh quick.'

Only a few moments passed and then Josh's larger shape loomed up before her. He peered through the darkness at her. 'Miss Hilliard, what on earth brings you here?'

'Listen!' she said. 'There isn't a moment to be lost. Captain Penn is on his way with a number of marines in addition to his own men. For heaven's sake, do what you can to get away.'

It was an emergency Josh had always allowed for and he wasted no time on questions. Accepting what she said as fact, he said to the nearest dark shape, 'Get every man back to the boat. Abandon everything. At the double now.' He turned back to Elise 'You're alone? How did you come?'

'Alone, yes. I rode Eddie's cob.' She gestured towards Brown Boy's bulky shadow.

'You can't go back that way. Penn will bring his men along the lane and his watchers will be on the shore path. You'll have to come with us.'

'But the cob?'

Josh stepped across to Brown Boy, undid buckles and had the saddle and reins off in moments. Leaving the bridle in place, he said to the man holding him, 'Turn him loose with the others and then get back to the boats as quick as you can.'

Having stuffed the reins into a capacious pocket, he heaved the saddle up on to one shoulder and grasping Elise by an arm, steered her rapidly towards the sea. 'Once the nag's with the others there'll be nothing to tell he wasn't one of the borrowed horses,' he told her. 'He'll be back in his stable before long, don't worry.'

Elise was aware of others hurrying along with them, all in silence. She was aware, too, of the bales and packages that were being abandoned making darker humps against the grassy track they were following. When they reached the edge of the land, two boats waited there, the black galley and a smaller dinghy, men already at the oars. Without ceremony, Josh lifted her into the galley, stepped in after her, and stowed away the saddle. Several more men joined them, the oars dipped and the galley pulled swiftly and strongly away into the darkness.

They came to the lugger suddenly, it seemed to Elise. Josh lifted her up to the deck-rail and into willing hands, whose owners then helped to steady her on her feet. The galley had a tow-rope attached and was pulled round to be fastened to *Sea Dancer*'s stern. Everything was done with a quiet efficiency that Elise found impressive. Within a few minutes the dinghy also reached the lugger. As the men in it scrambled aboard and hauled the boat up after them, the first sounds came to them from the land announcing the arrival of Penn and his men. *Sea Dancer*'s dark sails were already unfurled and she began to turn to take the wind. Shockingly loud across the water, came the sound of a shot.

'What the devil—' Josh swung round. 'Barney, is everyone on board?'

'Aboard and counted,' Barney answered out of the darkness.

Another man laughed. 'One of the lobster's shooting at shadows, for sure.'

'Lobsters?' Elise asked Josh still standing beside her, then staggered as the lugger dipped her bow.

Josh's arm shot out to prevent her falling. 'Marines,' he told her. 'Some seamen call them lobsters for their red coats.' He drew breath deeply into his lungs. 'Well, Miss Hilliard, here we are safe and sound and very much in your debt for it.'

'I'm sorry it meant losing your cargo. Though as a good citizen I have more than a strong suspicion I shouldn't be,' Elise said with a laugh, clinging tightly to a convenient rope to keep her balance.

'Oh, a good half was got away before you came. What's left will be sent to auction and what it fetches will be divided between those who were lucky enough to be there when it was found. Penn may not be all that happy about it, but the men will. The loss will be mine, so as a good citizen you could say the villain got his deserts.' He laughed, untroubled.

'But will it turn you from your wicked ways? Somehow I don't think so. And I should, perhaps, be worrying about having put myself in league with you, but I am more concerned to know how I am to get back to Greenaleigh.'

'Penn will have mustered all, or most,of his men for what he planned, which means he'll have few, if any, on watch close to his base. We'll stand off-shore a while to make sure there isn't a revenue cutter or such on watch, then I'll row you in and see you safe to Greenaleigh.' He leaned down a little as though to see her face more clearly. 'You seem to be a good sailor so far. How are you feeling?'

They were well under way and until now, she had given no thought to it. Thankfully she realized she had no sense of nausea. 'Fine,' she said. 'I feel fine.'

'This isn't quite what I meant when I promised you and Henry a sea trip,' Josh said with amusement 'Fortunately, the sea's running light tonight and *Sea Dancer* rides smoother than most thanks to a sharp prow and keel.' He was silent for a moment or two and Elise knew he was still staring down at her. Seriously now, he said, 'Grateful as I am, Miss Hilliard, it puzzles me why you, a young lady, should take the risks you have to come to our salvation.'

Why indeed? And how to answer him? For sorry though she would be to see disaster overtake Joshua Ryland, it had been for the sake of another man who might, or might not, have chosen to give him warning. Would he have stood by and seen Josh come to grief? She was less certain now than she had been that he would not. She gave Josh a roundabout answer to his question by describing Penn's late night visit to the vicarage but omitting to mention Mr Mariott's presence in the hall.

Josh was not so easily decoyed off course. 'That explains the circumstances, but not the reason. Why should you care?'

'There was no one else there who could warn you and no time to find someone. *And* you are Henry's friend,' she declared, feeling colour flare into her cheeks and praying that the night hid it from Josh.

Josh pursued it no further. He did not flatter himself that she had developed tender feelings towards him. Without vanity, he knew he was attractive to women and knew the signs. Whatever Miss Hilliard's reasons, she had more than earned the right to keep them to herself if she chose. 'Well, you're a high-couraged lady and no mistake,' he said. 'There are a good many families hereabouts with cause to be grateful to you tonight.' His voice lightened and amusement threading his words, he went on, 'As for myself, I must count myself more than fortunate to be Henry's friend.'

Soon after that, at a brief word of command from Josh, *Sea Dancer* was hove-to, the dinghy was lowered again and Elise lifted down into her. As though he could see in the dark, Josh rowed her unerringly towards the unseen shore, bringing the dinghy in to a point almost directly opposite the copse near Danesfield's stables where once she had stood in the sunrise and Nicholas Mariott had found her.

Once on land, with the cob's saddle slung over one shoulder, Josh guided her towards the trees, picked up the path to the lane and led her through to the gate giving on to it. Having made sure there was no one about and refusing to listen to any protest she made, he continued with her to the gates of Greenaleigh and up the drive past the house into the stableyard.

Immediately, Eddie Hammond appeared.

'Eddie!' Elise said exasperatedly. 'I told you not to come down again.'

'Well, I didn't, miss, because I didn't go up. Been waiting. You've been a prodigious long time though. I've been worried. And where's Brown Boy?' But it was Josh he was staring at while he spoke and it was Josh who answered him.

'The cob's been "borrowed" and you can guess why. If he does-n't make his own way back sooner, he'll be found with the others. There's nothing to connect Miss Hilliard with him. Here's his saddle and reins. Put them where they ought to be and then forget you've seen either of us. You'll do well to have heard and seen nothing this night. I'll just see Miss Hilliard safely into the house and then I'll be away.'

Penn spent the three days following the smuggling run in a fury of frustration, not in any way alleviated by *Sea Dancer*'s return on the evening of the second day laden with fish and not an item of contraband to be found on her anywhere. There was nothing to show that the 'catch' had been bought outright from the master of a ketch only too pleased to dispose of it with so little trouble.

Not only had Penn a failed undertaking to explain, but he had a dead man to account for. He was thankful it was a marine who had fired the fatal shot and not one of his own men. The man, Daniel Osborne, a carpenter at Jepson's boatyard, walking home from Sidlesham after visiting his married sister had been unfortunate enough to meet Penn's party on Long Lane near the point where the overgrown path Elise had followed joined it. Hard of hearing since birth and a little bemused by tiredness and the quantity of his sister's home-brewed he had taken, he had failed to hear the challenge thrown at him. When, in the darkness someone had laid rough hands on him, Osborne, with no understanding of what was happening, had fought back strongly. Seeing the struggle and sure they had found the smugglers, one of his fellow marines had shot him. There had been no intention to kill, but Osborne had died.

Penn drew no comfort for the night's work from the prospect of some financial gain from the sale of the abandoned contraband. What obsessed him was how Ryland and his gang had been alerted to the imminent arrival of his party. The possibility of Nicholas Mariott having broken his word took him to Danesfield to question its owner. The almost contemptuous dismissal of the implication did nothing to soothe the captain's feelings, but little as he wanted to, he was forced to believe Mariott spoke the truth. A brief interview with Sir Roland convinced him, too, that the magistrate had not made any careless mention of the impending ambush to his wife or to anyone else.

Working carefully through all possibilities, he remembered his last minute glimpse of Elise Hilliard and Mary Staunton at the top of the vicarage stairs. How long had they been there? How much had they heard? That either, dressed as they were and with so little time available, would or could have carried a warning to the smugglers seemed to him to be too unlikely. That was until one of his men relayed a story he had heard in the village. . . .

The tale went that Tom Forbes, walking back to Twitch-up Farm and the shelter of its hay-barn for the night, on hearing the approach of a fast ridden horse, had fallen into a hedge as he tried to put himself safely out of the way. The horse, he swore, had been ridden by a woman. He also swore he was sober, or nearly so.

It was known that Tom had spent the evening in the Sussex Oak having earned two shillings and his dinner at Twitch-up that day shovelling muck out of the pig-pen, so not too much credit was given to the story by those who knew him. The more so when he went on to say that the horse was a great black beast ridden astride by a wild-looking female in floating white garments. One of Tom's alcoholic dreams was the general opinion.

Penn, however, considered its possible truth. By no stretch of imagination could he see Mary Staunton riding through the night to warn smugglers of an impending raid; she was too proper, too conscious of her responsibility as the vicar's daughter. But Elise Hilliard? Unlikely but not impossible. And the gown she had been wearing was pale in colour, might even have been white. If she it was, she would have had to act quickly, there would have been no time to change clothes. What her motive could have been he could not guess and cared not at all, but it would give him great satisfaction to bring it home to her. Not least for the humiliation of the occasion when Nicholas Mariott had found him with the girl struggling in his arms.

The fact that the Greenaleigh cob had been found in the early morning waiting patiently outside the gates to the house for someone to open them meant little unless taken with the rest. It was no 'great black beast', but that could be put down to Forbes's drunken exaggeration. None of it amounted to much, but in the absence of any other line to follow, Penn thought it enough to allow him to give Miss Hilliard an uncomfortable hour or two. He might even fluster her into making a damaging admission.

Summoned to Cousin Matthew's study in the late afternoon, Elise, entered the room with no expectation of trouble. But when she saw Matthew was not alone and recognized who it was who stood in close conversation with him, she felt the chill touch of premonition.

Penn asked his questions with cold courtesy and was answered in the same manner. Elise had no choice but to deny absolutely that she had warned the smugglers of Penn's approach, or, indeed, had any knowledge of a run being made until it was the talk of the village. Nor could she be shaken from that stand.

Penn's failure to ruffle her calm, pushed him unreasonably into angry certainty of her guilt. With time so short, she must have had the use of a horse – which fell in with Tom Forbes's story. He asked Matthew to send for the groom.

Though Eddie might wonder why Miss Hilliard should ally herself with the smugglers, he was born and bred in Elswick which alone ensured his loyalty even if it was not committed to Miss Hilliard for her own sake. When he understood what Penn was about, he held staunchly to having seen nothing, heard nothing, known nothing of Brown Boy's disappearance on the night of the smuggling run until he was discovered in the morning. This was a standard claim by anyone who had horses borrowed by the smugglers and would be a waste of time to dispute, though Penn tried.

There was nothing to be gained by prolonging the interview. Penn ended it by informing Matthew that since no one could positively vouch for Miss Hilliard not having left the house after returning from the Colbrookes with her cousins, it would be necessary to take her to the watch-house to meet a witness who might possibly identify her as the woman he had seen riding towards where the contraband had been found.

'I think, sir,' he told Matthew, with every appearance of sympathetic gravity, 'that you must be prepared for the probability that I shall have to lay a formal charge against Miss Hilliard before Sir Roland.'

192

Matthew had no idea whether Penn was acting within the limits of his authority in what he proposed and his protests were wavering and ineffectual. He looked at his young cousin with wondering uncertainty. Could she have done as Penn suspected? And above all, *why* would she? She had denied it firmly enough, but in the months she had lived at Greenaleigh he had come to recognize that under her quiet good-humour there lay a valiant spirit. If she saw a good reason to do a thing, she would do it. But in this case. . . ?

There was nothing Elise could do but live through what was happening as best she could and maintain her innocence. To weaken would be to give Penn confirmation that the smugglers had been local men. She had not heard the Tom Forbes story and she wondered who it was claimed to have seen her and whether Penn could prove the charge he was making. Whether he could or not, she sensed that under his overt courtesy he was enjoying himself. She wrapped the shawl Betty brought around herself and walked out of the house beside Penn with what dignity she could.

Amelia had no difficulty in believing in Elise's guilt when Matthew told her what had happened. It was her shrill diatribe against the shame Elise's bold, unprincipled behaviour had brought to the household that gave Henry a fairly clear picture of what had happened. His immediate response was to slip out of the house and head for Danesfield. Uncle Nick had rescued both Saul Wadey and Andy from Captain Penn: Henry had no doubt he could do as much for Cousin Elise.

Nick, however, was not to be found at Danesfield. He had ridden in to Bognor and the time of his return was uncertain. Henry poured out his tale into Landers' sympathetic ear and was promised his godfather would be given the news the minute he returned.

It was a full half-hour later before Nick came back to Danesfield and darkness had fallen before he reached the house. Landers faithfully relayed Henry's tale. The strength of his master's reaction to it, if judged by the expression that first crossed his face, gave Landers something extra to think about.

Nick had walked away from the butler unconscious of direction. He found he had entered the bookroom and shutting the door behind him, leaned against it while he considered what he had been told. He found even less difficulty than Penn in believing Elise Hilliard capable of recklessly setting out to rescue Joshua Ryland and the rest from invited disaster. She must have heard what Penn said to Sir Roland when he called at the vicarage. What quixotic idea could have motivated the foolish, meddlesome girl this time? 'For Henry's sake' hardly seemed sufficient for *this*. And what an instrument of revenge she had handed Penn!

For all his angry condemnation of what she had done, he had known from the moment Landers had passed on Henry's message that he would move heaven and earth to extricate her from this scrape in which she had landed herself. The only question was where to start? Neither appeal nor argument would move Penn this time, he was sure. The man had a score to settle. But if he could reach Sir Roland before Penn, supposing Penn succeeded in pushing the matter that far, he might gain the ear of that amenable magistrate and avert the worst.

He had no time to waste on further speculation and deciding that he could reach the manor as quickly on foot as by horse, he set out at once. Walking at a brisk pace down the few hundred yards from Danesfield towards the village, he was headed for the footpath that crossed the small green there. It would take him along one side of the Sussex Oak and from there he had only to cross the lane to the manor-house gates.

Wrapped in worried thought, he was attempting to marshal the arguments he might need to lay before Sir Roland to gain his support. He neither heard nor sensed the presence of the man who had followed him from the time he left Danesfield until, as he reached the deeper shadow of the inn's side wall, something hard jabbed him between the shoulder blades.

'Go into the Oak through the side door there, *Mister* Mariott,' Josh's voice said over his shoulder. Then grittily, as Nick attempted to turn, 'No argument! This time, I'm the one holding a pistol.'

A vigorous nudge persuaded Nick to obey and he walked through the door indicated into the narrow passage that led between the taproom on the right and the little used coffee-room and the kitchen on the left. Tonight the coffee-room door stood ajar on a room bright with lamplight and the glimmer of a drift-wood fire. Pushed towards this, Nick walked forward with quick, angry steps. The rasp of a key in the lock of the door swung him round to find he was facing one of the new naval pistols held squarely pointing at him. His first thought was that whatever Josh wanted he could not have chosen a more evil-hour in which to present it. His mind in turmoil and seething with impatience, Nick said, 'For whatever reason I'm here, tell me quickly; I'm in a hurry.'

'Too bad, because you're going nowhere.'

That jolted him sufficiently to turn his thoughts from Elise to full awareness of here and now. Josh was watching him closely, his eyes glittering, expectant. With a sense of shock, Nick drew the parallel between the present situation and what had happened between them at Danesfield. It was the situation reversed. Then, the focus of Josh's anguished concern had been Andy; now, for him, it was Elise. So completely had he rethought his attitude to Josh, he had lost sight of the improbability of Josh having made a similar adjustment. It came back to him now with devastating force and he recollected the quiet earnestness of Josh's vow to kill him.

Josh's gaze had narrowed sharply as he watched Nick's changing expression. His smile taking on a tigerish quality, softly, tauntingly, he asked, 'Had you thought I'd forgotten?'

Nick said urgently, 'Josh, listen!'

'Shouldn't it be *Ryland*?'

The stinging sarcasm of that told Nick how false his accidental use of the old familiar name had sounded in Josh's ears. Now, at

195

an even greater disadvantage, deep in frustration, he said, 'Damn all that! You *have* to listen to me!'

Josh's smile grew more tigerish and he gave the pistol a slight lift. 'This says I don't. And it isn't your leg it's aimed at. We've both made mistakes, one about the other, haven't we? But make no mistake about that.'

With wicked deliberation he cocked the pistol.

CHAPTER TWENTY

In the silence that followed, seconds seemed to lengthen into eternity as they stared at each other across the small distance that separated them. Then, recollecting Elise, everything else dropped out of mind and Nick said with the same unthinking urgency as before, 'Josh, listen—'

Josh's lip curled. 'Oh, no, don't grovel! I remember a boy who'd have said, *Shoot, and be damned!*'

'If you'd just *hear* me—'

'No. You hear *me*. The story goes that it was an unknown assailant who came close to robbing me of this happy opportunity. But you *did* know who it was, didn't you?' Anger throbbed through the final question.

Nick was silenced.

A surge of naked fury swept away Josh's humour, dark as it was. 'You made Andy swear not to tell me. Well, now the boy's forsworn. When his brooding began to worry his mother, I gave him notice either he told me what he was mumping over or I'd thrash it out of him. It will probably please you to know he let me get well started before he broke!'

Nick sensed the pain behind those words . . . recognized the unforgivable offence. 'No,' he said, and shook his head at what was beyond explaining. 'I'm sorry it came to that.'

'Hell take it, you're sorry!' The words were barbed with scorn-

197

ful grievance. 'He all but killed you but Hammond and Young Pete were there and Andy says he didn't run. He was in their grasp. And through them, in *yours*. You had witnesses. Could have had him charged with attempted murder . . . hanged, jailed, transported for life. . . . Damn you! And damn you again! What twisted undergame has held you in check? Having Andy, you had me . . . Prue . . . *all* my family under your hand.'

Stung beyond bearing, sense departed and Nick said thinly, 'I still do,' the words as wicked in intent as Josh's cocking of the pistol had been.

For a formidable moment Josh did not speak. Then, softly: 'So you do. But for how much longer?' The baleful silence returned, beat timelessly about them until Josh, his voice leaden said, 'When I heard about the attack on you, I never thought it might be Andy. Had no idea the boy—' He let that go. Went on, 'I tell you I *wanted* you dead. Thought—'

That final injurious straw ripped the last shred of caution from Nick and he slashed across Josh's words, 'Then make sure of it now! Else, I'm coming past you.'

Tension pulsed on snapping point again. Then Josh said, 'By God, you tempt me to oblige you, Nicholas Mariott!'

It was a different voice. Quiet. Tired. Bleak with a bitterness to equal his own. Nick's black gaze came back from distance to refocus on Josh's face.

'If you'd heard me out – I might have *thought* I wanted you dead, but I found myself praying you'd live. And not because I was hell-bent on keeping the pleasure of killing you for myself. Damn you to hell for believing so, whatever I may have said.' He shook his head exasperatedly. 'And damn you again for standing there, *goading* me to do it!'

Nick made a gesture of repudiation. 'No. It wasn't intended.' But it took time to accept the rest, to readjust to the illogicality of it. Illogical but human. He drew breath, said slowly, 'Nothing in the past months . . . or here tonight . . . gave me reason to think otherwise.'

198

'Tonight? Tonight your expectation was writ so large on your face, I thought I'd allow you full enjoyment of it.'

With an effort, Nick swallowed that, a small sound that was not quite a laugh escaping him. 'And while you continue to point that pistol at me, I suppose I shall.'

Josh glanced at the weapon with something like surprise, uncocked it and slid it into his belt.

'I needed to make you listen to me and it seemed' – a flicker of humour – 'appropriate. But then' – he shrugged – 'things got out of hand. The way they do.'

Nick nodded.

'The boy . . . he never intended your death.' Josh's tone demanded understanding. 'Blame *me*. I didn't want to talk about what happened that night. Didn't tell him enough to satisfy him. *That*, and knowing you'd shot me, gnawed at him until he was driven to go to your house with one of the wild and muddled ideas that afflict boys of his age. He thought to confront you, to make *you* tell him. But you weren't at Danesfield. He wandered down to the stables with nothing clear in his mind. Then he heard you coming, stepped into one of the boxes and found himself trapped in the dark between you and that demon-horse of yours. When you wrestled him, he struck out.'

'Yes, I know. Guessed. Josh, if there's more it will have to wait—'

'There's more and it can't wait, Nick. I'm off to France on tonight's tide which is not far off. I won't be back until the Blockade's lifted, so I'll not be here to plague you much longer.' He grimaced. 'Too much is changing. Young Osborne being killed. Uphman giving up. Others thinking of it. But above all, the family. Penn's a threat to them. Will use any means to reach me.'

'So what will you do?'

'I shall continue to trade, no doubt about that.' His voice lightened, took on its familiar edge of laughter. 'It's in the blood. Think about it, Nick. You and I, we both do what we were born to do, what our fathers did. You on the land. Me on the sea. The

Blockade's had some success, but nothing like what bringing down taxes would do. The navy's broken many of the big, wild gangs, but small bands like mine still slip in and out. With the Turks giving trouble, the navy'll be needed to stop their caper. The government's run ships and men down so far, they're already calling back some of those manning the Blockade. Things may be easier yet.'

Nick could look at him now with affectionate understanding: an adventurer through and through, and, as he said, born to it, bred to it. He was too, a man who drew the loyalty not only of his own men but the many villagers who benefited from what he did one way or another. He was not the only leader of a smuggling band to have his name blessed by those among whom he lived, and of those others there were several who could not claim reputations free from violence or even murder. As he did not doubt that Josh – outside any threat to his family – could. As for the many who accepted his largesse, when choice lay starkly between starvation and accepting the generosity of an outlaw, the choice was easy.

'So you'll be living in France?' Nick said. 'It's hard to imagine.'

'I might even become a Frenchie. For a time. If I run into trouble over here then, all they can do is send me back to France. Think of that!'

'A more unlikely Frenchman I've yet to see.'

'Some even more unlikely are already there. Five hundred at Qimper. I speak the language well enough to get by and it's a fair country. The French welcome us. Make it easy. Even provide men to make up a crew. They'll never love the English, but they love English gold. They've called us a nation of shopkeepers. They should know: grandmothers are two a penny over there.'

'So Prue and the boys are going with you?'

'Yes. But not tonight. I'll find a home for them first. I'm leaving Andy to be the man of the family for now. What I wanted to ask you was if you'd keep an eye open for them all until I send. Maybe see them safe on to a cross-channel packet?'

200

Nick laughed. 'You have the gall to ask it after what you've put me through tonight?'

'Well, I've taken a few wounds from that viper's tongue of yours, Nick Mariott.'

Their gaze met and held in mockery and challenge. Then Nick said, 'I'll bring them safe across the channel to you. I'd have done as much even if you had not asked.'

Josh nodded easy acceptance. 'There's more.'

'Go on.'

'I went to Chichester yesterday. To your bank and mine. Made a sum of money over to your care. Signed papers. There's some waiting for you to sign. This list' – he pulled out some papers from an inner pocket and selected one – 'I suppose you could call 'em pensioners. Elswick men who came to grief smuggling. Their families mostly. If you'd see they get their money regular.'

There were five names on the list, the last one covering the widow and the two small children of the man who had been killed in Penn's ambush. Nick took in the capital sum, said, 'You must be a rich man, Josh, to afford this.

The laughter in Josh's voice deepened. 'My father did not leave me poor and I've added my mite to that. There should be enough and more to cover. If not, let me know.'

Nick stared down at the list.'You did all this before you saw me this evening.'

'Well. . . .'

Sensing the shrug that accompanied the single word, Nick looked up. Blue gaze again met brown, this time in mutual acknowledgement. The bond might have frayed, it had not broken.

'You made me so damned furious,' Josh offered unexpectedly. 'I'd always led and you followed. It touched my pride and that damned tongue of yours did the rest. *A lesser man than you'd thought me.* . . . I valued your opinion and those words did damage. And then the black boat on the night of the storm. . . . Your cursed generosity. God, how I wanted to punish you for that!'

'You did, Josh. Take my word for it. But now . . . all accounts squared?'

'All but the greatest. For Andy, I give you your lady.'

'My lady?'

'Miss Hilliard. Eddie Hammond knew what she did . . . saddled the horse by which she came to warn us. He had the wit to let me know what had happened to her. Do you think I could let it rest after she had saved our necks?'

'But Penn had her . . . was taking her to Sir Roland to charge her with obstructing a King's Officer in the performance of his duty. It was what I was trying to tell you at the beginning.'

'I know. But I didn't mean to let you.'

'*You* – no, damn you, I refuse to rise to that. How did you get her away from Penn?'

'I sent him a message offering the kind of bargain he likes: myself in exchange for Miss Hilliard. I let Penn think what he likes to think, that the peasant had raised his eyes above his station. Was love-smitten. He snapped at it. I made one condition – he and the lady met me alone. I was certain enough that Penn would have some trickery up his sleeve so I just made sure he had no time to use it. As soon as the captain and Miss Hilliard were at a safe distance from the watch-house, I had a sack over the captain's head, his pistol in my hand and a rope round his arms. A leaf out of his own book, so to speak. I took Miss Hilliard to Prue, dumped Penn in my gig-shed, well trussed. He'll be taking a short trip in *Sea Dancer* with me tonight.'

'*But Elise* . . . Miss Hilliard. In what state is she? And why did she do it . . . take such risk?'

'You should ask her. Not for my sake, so don't think it.'

'Is she still at your cottage?'

'Unless she's in the gig with Andy and Prue and on her way here, that's where she is. She's taken no great harm, don't fret.'

Nick's relief was beyond words. He spared a thought for Penn. A flawed man who took short cuts to success. 'What do you intend for the captain? Not tipping him overboard halfway across the channel?'

202

'A temptation, but no. I'll land him at Brest. Lose him some-where in the country beyond Qimper probably. He can arrange his own return. How long that will take depends on how much money he has in his pocket, how well he speaks the language, how persuasive he is.' He was laughing openly now. 'I doubt persuasion is one of Penn's talents. My guess is he'll take longer than most to get home. And don't concern yourself about Miss Hilliard. Penn had no time to reach Sir Roland and lay any charge against her. When the captain gets back to this country, he'll be too busy explaining himself to his commanding officer to busy himself with Miss Hilliard. I'll be gone and the likely chance is they'll put someone else in his place here so when he gets back he'll be sent elsewhere.'

Everything seemed to have been said, but now Josh was look-ing at him with a quizzical amusement that made Nick demand suspiciously, 'Well?'

'Oh, just a small thing. . . . Given your certainty I intended your death, what did you think Ben Saulter would say to finding Mr Mariott dead on his coffee-room floor?'

Nick looked blank for a moment. Then, 'The room had been prepared . . . I supposed . . . I don't know, I didn't think beyond the impression that made.' He shrugged. 'You're more valuable to Ben than I could be.'

Josh laughed and shook his head. 'Oh, indeed! How could Nicholas Mariott weigh with Ben against a score or so of cheap half-ankers of brandy a year? I should admire to see his face if you asked him.'

He was about to add to that but a knock on the door inter-rupted. No ordinary knock, a signal. Josh turned and unlocked it. Elise, Prue and Andy came in escorted by Ben Saulter himself. Having nodded his brindled head at the two men, the innkeeper discreetly returned to his own affairs.

Prue Ryland entered first. She looked at her husband, her brows rising slightly in enquiry. Josh gave the smallest nod. Prue smiled.

Walking to meet Prue, Nick was looking at Elise and missed the

203

exchange between husband and wife. He was still looking at her when, observing a long-standing privilege, he bent to kiss Prue's cheek. He took note of the girl's pallor and that both her gown and shawl were a little soiled. No harm, but what indignities had Penn thrust on her? At that moment he felt a strong urge to undertake to tip Penn into mid-channel himself.

He went from Prue to Elise who regarded him warily before saying as though he had spoken, 'Yes. I fell into trouble again, but please don't scold. Or not yet.'

There was a poignancy in that out-of-character admission of weakened defences that touched him deeply. But what she saw as his likely response to her situation was both wounding and humbling.

He said almost harshly, 'Is a scold the best you can expect from me? Yes. I suppose it is. I can only say it was not in my mind. I wanted – had hoped to be of some service to you.'

'Mr Nicholas.' Prue claimed his attention again. 'I'm sorry, but Josh and me, we don't have much time and Andy is here because he has something to say to you.'

Andy's expression was a mixture of apprehension and 15-year-old defiance.

Nick looked at him and smiled. 'You don't need to say it, Andy. It was dark in the stable. I don't believe you intended to kill me.'

That unexpected subvention brought Andy's guard down. 'I – I only wanted to speak to you, but the horse was snorting and kicking and I heard the others coming. It was too much. I was afraid.' He stared at Nick, all his young doubt of adult understanding in his face. 'I couldn't see you, but I knew who you were. I'd heard you speak to the horse. I wouldn't have done it, but you had me by the throat.'

'And perhaps you were not entirely averse to giving me something to remember you by . . . justice as you saw it.'

'Not really. I just wanted to escape,' Andy said, with painful honesty.

'Why then did you not run afterwards when you had clear

opportunity? You must have known your father would have got you away. To France. To America.'

'John Hammond had a lantern. When I saw – when I saw what I—' The boy's eyes closed momentarily as though to shut out the memory. He shook his head. 'I thought I *had* killed you.'

'All the more reason to run, surely?'

'I couldn't! I felt—' He shook his head wildly. 'I didn't want you to die. You'd been *my* friend, too.'

'Thank you, Andy. That's recompense enough. Forget the rest.'

If Andy did not altogether understand, Josh did. Over his son's shoulder, he gave Nick a brief, appreciative nod. Then said, 'We must be off. The nag's waiting and the tide will be on the turn before long.' He held out a large hand. 'I'll see you from time to time, Nick. Mostly on dark nights. Some of the men who'll be coming with me tonight will be back. The married men. Maybe to turn farmers on your scheme. The rest, like myself, won't come until times are easier.'

Nick grasped the hand warmly. 'Good luck, Josh. If you do ever want to turn farmer—'

He laughed. 'Oh, no. Not me. Too tame. The sea . . . the trade. It's the only life for me. If I end with my head in a noose, at least I'll have lived the way I choose.' He shrugged, grinned. 'Meanwhile, I shall look to borrow horses from law-abiding land-lubbers on occasion.'

'Don't ever think of borrowing Rahu.'

'My need is for *useful* beasts, not devils on four legs.'

On his way to the door, Josh paused beside Elise and held out his hand again. 'You and I have said all we need I think, Miss Hilliard, except that I'm proud to have met you. I hope we'll meet again.' He lowered his voice. 'Take him in hand.' He gave a small jerk of his head towards Nick. 'Teach him to laugh more. He had laughter bullied out of him when he was a lad.' A smiling nod and he was gone, followed by his wife and son.

*

When the door had closed on the Rylands, Nick looked again at Elise. She gazed back at him doubtfully, weary-looking, vulnerable. He took in the sweetness visible in her face; thought of her courage, her honesty, her generosity. And he the fool who had deliberately closed his eyes to those qualities because of an old disappointment and because one of his father's many harangues had got through to him in a weak moment.He felt a pain that was almost physical, ached to take her in his arms, comfort her . . . comfort himself. But he had thrown away any chance he might have had with her. *His lady. . . ?* Josh could not have meant what his words implied, but with all his heart he wished she were indeed his lady. Of the several things urgent to be spoken, out a depth of irrepressible feeling, he said what his reasoning mind was least likely to have chosen.

'I love you.'

The ghost of her lovely smile curved her lips. 'Are you sure?'

It was so unexpected a response he snapped back unthinkingly, 'Of course I'm sure, or I should not say so!' And then in sheerest exasperation 'You are the darnedest woman—!'

The smile wavered, became half apologetic.. 'I think there has been some uncertainty. I appeared to give you so many reasons to disapprove of me. Even to dislike me. I interfered between you and Mr Ryland . . . was foolish enough to allow myself to be trapped by Captain Penn that night at the Colbrookes.'

He said unhappily, 'I have been something much worse than foolish. It would not surprise me to find you can only think of me with contempt.'

'That sounds as though you are about to abandon the field. Such a pity after having made such a brave beginning.'

'Yes. I deserve to be laughed at.'

'I am not laughing at you. To the contrary, I have just opened the way for you to continue from where you began. How did you mean to go on from "I love you" if I had not said the wrong thing?'

He said ruefully, 'I had no plan. It was the expression of a wish . . . a deep longing. To sweep you off your feet, perhaps. To make irresistible love to you.'

'It is odd, but I think I could be very easily swept off my feet.'

'I wish I could believe you mean that.'

'I am sorry you so doubt what I say. In general, I am very truthful.'

She was looking at him with a tenderness in her eyes about which he surely could not be mistaken. He moved closer, hope bringing his hands up to grasp her shoulders.

'Are you so?' he said, his voice rough with emotion. 'Don't tease, I beg. Just tell me – could you love me?'

'I do.'

He gave a short incredulous bark of laughter. Shook his head, said unbelievingly, 'Enough to marry me?'

'Yes.'

'Just like that. With no more loverlike protestations from me?'

Her eyes were sparkling with laughter now. 'I shall expect some future evidence of your affection, of course.'

'By heaven you shall have it!' On a fierce upthrust of happiness, he pulled her close and Elise raised her face for his kiss, her lips as eager as his.